A Second Chance

To Abe

[signature] 10/18/2008

COMMENTS:

"A Second Chance" has provided a personal blessing to me from the Holy Spirit as well as deepened my knowledge-base in my walk in faith with the Lord Jesus Christ. This book is truly a witness by Pastor DeGraft-Amanfu to the power, grace and tender mercies of our Lord Jesus Christ. May God bless each and every one of you in your new walk with Him.

—Jan Montoya

A Second Chance

"Come to me, all you who labor and are heavy laden, and I will give you rest" (Matthew 11:28 NKJV)

Joseph Degraft-Amanfu

DEDICATION

To my Lord and blessed Savior Jesus Christ, I dedicate this book. How impossible will it be if the blessed Holy Spirit had not been the source, helper, and instructor? To God the Father I owe my soul, spirit, and body.

May my life continue to be a perpetual sacrifice to Him and His Church, the body of Christ. May God pour me forth as a drink offering to the thirsty and patched souls of men who languish for the truth.

Again, I dedicate this book to students of all ages, Sunday Schools of all denominations, Scripture unions, Student fellowships, Boys and girls' scouts, youth groups, parents who desire to see their children and loved ones saved, and Christians who are experiencing doubts concerning their Salvation.

May the blessings of the Lord be upon you as you read this book, Amen.

THANKS

Many thanks to my dear and precious wife Miranda, for her great sacrifice and contribution while preparing this book. The countless nights she had to spend alone while I was burning the midnight oil are forever cherished.

I am particularly thankful to Denise Harrison (my secretary), Hannah Blango, Reverend Anthony Amoako, Pastor Sylvia Allotey, and most importantly, Editor Jan Montoya and Senior Editor Stephen Bess, for their valuable contributions in editing and getting this book ready for publishing.

May the Lord bless and prosper the body of Christ who worship at the Anointed Church of God, Beltsville, Maryland, United States for their support, contribution, and prayer.

Last but not least, I give thanks to my lovely daughters Melanie and Adwoa, for all the drinks and delicious food that kept my brain working at full capacity throughout the preparation of this precious book.

CONTENTS

Introduction xv

Chapter One: Man as he was Made 1
Chapter Two: The Fall of Man 13
Chapter Three: The Heart of God 31
Chapter Four: What God has already Done 45
Chapter Five: From Faith to Faith 89
Chapter Six: New Man 107
Chapter Seven: New Boss 119
Chapter Eight: Conflict 125
Chapter Nine: More than a Conqueror 131
Chapter Ten: Glorified 137
Chapter Eleven: My Testimony 143

INTRODUCTION

One great truth I learned in my walk with God is that, God can use any vessel that is yielded and willing. For me, writing this book was a task far beyond my capability; "Who am I to write a book on the most controversial and important need of all mankind?", I asked myself. I felt inadequate and ill-prepared. Right from the beginning, I knew this was God at work. I also knew the only way to get this book out to His people was to completely yield to His sway; to be the vessel ready for the master's use.

This book is the outcome of many months of prayer and dedication. Being aware of the many lives that will be imparted, I prayed earnestly for divine guidance and wisdom. I sought the help of the Holy Spirit more than ever. I present the truth of God's word not as a professional in a secular sense, but as a servant still learning and taking instruction, from the master. My prayer is that you do not judge this book by its grammar, or modest style of presentation. Having had struggles of my own, I seek to humbly make available to all what God has asked me to do.

Men don't live forever; hence, my prayer is that this book will become a tool in the hands of His people, for the equipping of the saints, and for the work of evangelism now and generations to come. We must study to show ourselves approved unto God and ready to fulfill the great commission (Matthew 28:19). It is our duty to get past the doubts and fears surrounding our salvation and reach out to the many who are not Saved.

Everyone is good enough for heaven. The will of God is that all men (male and female) be saved and come to the knowledge of the truth. I pray that anyone who picks up this book and reads it will become a Christian; and if not, at least know what it takes to be a Christian. I seek not to congratulate myself for having achieved this, but I hope you will let me know if I did when we meet in glory.

Again, I pray this book will answer the cry of the many who are saved, born again, or Christians, but are not sure. A lesson I learned earlier in my career as an itinerant teacher of God's word is not to take anything for granted. In many cases, what I thought was simple and understood by every Christian, to my surprise was not. May this book settle every doubt and give you all the assurance you need for your Salvation.

If you are concerned for a loved one who is not saved, then this book is a perfect gift. This book is also a perfect gift to you because it will deepen your understanding and relationship with God. Finally, may all who read this book share it with anyone who has not. God has given each of us a second chance; this means including you.

Chapter One

MAN
AS HE WAS MADE

God made the world. God is directly responsible for the creation and sustenance of the universe through the agency of His Word. God has always existed and is distinct from His creation. Creation was a once and for all event, a completed act. Man did not just evolve; he is not nature's mistake, God created man:

"In the beginning God created the heaven and the earth" (Genesis 1:1; cf. Psalm 124:8).

"I have made the earth, and created man upon it: I, even my hands, have stretched out the heavens, and all their host have I commanded" (Isaiah 45:12).

"Who hath measured the waters in the hollow of his hand, and meted out heaven with the span, and comprehended the dust of the earth in a measure, and weighed the mountains in scales, and the hills in a balance?" (Isaiah 40:12; cf. 42:5).

God is one in his essential being; but in this being, there are three persons: the Father, the Son, and the Holy Spirit. This means there are three persons, but one God

(Deuteronomy 6:4). The Father is a person and fully God, the Son is a person and fully God and the Holy Spirit is a person and fully God. One without the other is not God and God without the others is not God. The question of a Three-In-One God (Trinity) transcends reason and may have to be accepted only by faith. The three-in-one God created both the universe and mankind:

> "Go ye therefore, and teach all nations, baptizing them in the name of the Father, and of the Son, and of the Holy Ghost" (Matthew 28:19).

> "The spirit of God hath made me, and the breath of the Almighty hath given me life" (Job 33:4).

> "For unto us a child is born, unto us a son is given: and the government shall be upon his shoulder: and his name shall be called Wonderful, Counsellor, The mighty God, The everlasting Father, The Prince of Peace" (Isaiah 9:6; cf. John 1:1-3).

> "The grace of the Lord Jesus Christ, and the love of God, and the communion of the Holy Ghost, be with you all. Amen" (2 Corinthians 13:14).

Man is the crown of God's creation. God created man in His own image and likeness. The creation of man was a separate act; His creation was special. He was made with deliberation and counsel. The statement, "let us make man in our image, after our likeness" testifies to man's noble creation:

> "And God said, Let us make man in our image, after our likeness: and let them have dominion over the fish of the sea, and over the fowl of the air, and over the cattle, and over all the earth, and over every creeping thing that creepeth upon the earth.

So God created man in his own image, in the image of God created he him; male and female created he them" (Genesis 1:26-27; cf. Job 10:8-11; 12:10; 33:4).

Apart from man, everything we see around us was simply called into being. With man, God actually went to work. Like the potter, he fashioned us with His own hands. "But now, O LORD, thou art our father; we are the clay, and thou our potter; and we all are the work of thy hand" (Isaiah 64:8). The making of man was in this form; first, there was the assembling of materials from the earth, and then, a simultaneous in-breathing of lives to form a soul or man:

"And the LORD God formed man of the dust of the ground, and breathed into his nostrils the breath of life; and man became a living soul" (Genesis 2:7).

The union of Spirit and body produced a living soul or a living, physical being. Man is therefore a tripartite being made up of spirit, soul, and body (1 Thessalonians 5:23). He was carefully made with a part that was spiritual or heavenly, and a part that was of the earthly or physical. The spiritual immaterial part was necessary for immortality, morality, and divine fellowship. The earthly part was to enable him to rule with compassion, administer justice, and care for the lower order. Further, man's earthly part was to ignite in him a responsible attitude towards the plant world from which his earthly frame depends. Man's spiritual and physical nature was a completed and simultaneous act.

Made in the 'image and likeness of God' distinguishes man from all other creatures and enables him to effectively relate to his Creator. Man has a moral and spiritual resemblance to God his maker. Unlike the other creatures, man was created with exceptional abilities to reason, love, plan, and exercise his own will. God blessed man with intelligible speech and the capacity to worship. It is this image and likeness to God that gives man his worth or weightiness and not in the abundance and superfluity of material possessions, education, and illustrious ancestry.

"Likeness and image of God" also made man a creature of faith. This is a characteristic peculiar only to mankind. Man, like his maker, can call forth those things which be not as though they were (Romans 4:17). He can dream, receive intimation, visions and communicate them in speech, writing, and exhibit his achievement. Man before the fall had absolute faith in God; meaning, he had the faith of God or the God kind of faith.

The works of Jesus and Adam before his fall are classic examples of what faith in God can do. Can you imagine Adam gave names to every living creature on earth? If one wants to know exactly how dignified man was made, then one must take a look at Jesus. He is our role model and perfect example. His power over nature, quality of faith and purity of life is how man was made. He is man as he was originally made by the hands of his God. Thanks to God one day all believers will be made like Jesus; man will get a second chance (1John 3:2):

> **"And out of the ground the LORD God formed every beast of the field, and every fowl of the air; and brought them unto Adam to see what he would call them: and whatsoever Adam called every living creature, that was the name thereof.**

> **And Adam gave names to all cattle, and to the fowl of the air, and to every beast of the field; but for Adam there was not found an help meet for him"** **(Genesis 2:19-20).**

Noah by faith built the first cruise ship, a three story ship. By faith he brought two of every sort of living creature into the ship. There was no indication he was an animal expert or had prior experience in ship building. He simply took God at his word and acted on it (Genesis 6:14-16). Noah's faith is another example of man as he was created. Man as he was made was full of faith.

Man is a personal being. God made man's body, frame or the external physical part out of the fine dust of the earth. The body connects us with the world or our environment through the five senses of hearing, seeing, smelling, tasting, and feeling. The soul or the man represents self-consciousness possessing heart, mind and will. God gave part of Himself to man, and God "breathed into his nostrils the breath of life" (Genesis 2:7).

God is Spirit, regenerated man is also spirit (John 4:24). Breath or the spirit, the immaterial part of man is like the wind, it is invisible, immaterial and powerful (John 3:8). Spirit is the element in man which gives him the ability to think of God or fellowship with God; it is his God-consciousness. Within man's inner self there is also the conscience, the faculty that distinguishes between right and wrong.

It is true that some animals can mimic or display traces of speech and intelligence, but that in no way compares with man who was purposely created to have fellowship with His maker and servant only to Him. No animal is said to have faith. Created to rule, man has the capacity for spirituality and goodness.

He has the ability to comb the ocean bed, search the sky, and the crust of the earth; the natural habitats of the fish, birds and other living things are part of his stewardship. It is man's duty to protect and ensure the well being of these creatures and to protect their habitats.

Man was created perfect and complete. He was created with moral obligations as well as physical responsibilities (Ecclesiastes 7:29). Unlike his maker, he could not "create," meaning, to make from "nothing;" but he was permitted to use and transform things made for his wellbeing. For example, he can get electricity from the wind, the sun, and water. He can make cars and planes to facilitate his journey from place to place.

One great wonder in man's creation is the gift of "free-will." Man as a personal being could make moral and immoral choices and be fully responsible for his choice. That is, man is the monarch of all that he surveys. He is culpable for what he says and does. Created to rule and king over the earth, he was responsible for his actions. Truly we can agree with the Psalmist, we are fearfully and wonderfully made: marvelous are thy works . . . (Psalm 139:14). Man is a creature of initiatives, enterprising, and creative powers.

The amazing power of 'free-will' is the freedom to choose to obey or disobey God. I believe this gift is what made the planting of the two trees in the Garden of Eden much more necessary and a revelation of divine wisdom. Man, invested with the power of creativity, moral goodness and uprightness, ruler of the lower creatures, with responsibility to subdue the earth and servant only to God, must be given the opportunity to prove his allegiance to divine authority. What will be the use of free-will with no freedom to choose?

Avertedly, man with this gift could make the earth a paradise or set it on fire. Life or death was for man to decide. We must never forget that free-will may not be freedom after all if we fail to use it wisely or as intended. We must be extremely cautious about the choices we make in life and with full understanding that the choices we individually make will determine our rise or fall. Some choices are forever, and others can be amended.

Further still, man's uniqueness is to enable him to function as God's representative, and acting on His behalf in His newly formed earth. Part of man's responsibility is to reign over the fish of the sea, the birds of the air, and over every living creature that moves upon the earth. The fear of animals and vice versa was instituted only after the fall (Genesis 9:2).

God blessed man saying:

"Be fruitful, and multiply, and replenish the earth, and subdue it: and have dominion over the fish of the sea, and over the fowl of the air, and over every living thing that moveth upon the earth" (Genesis 1:28).

Created as a king or ruler, man was specifically instructed to subdue and cultivate the fruitful earth. Every human being is entitled to share in the earth's resources. We must, therefore ensure and respect our neighbor's right to work, rest, obtain food, clothing and a descent shelter. The best and good things in life are for all to share. Each of us has a relationship and a responsibility to earth, which is a God given mandate.

Man like his Creator was created a social being. He is commanded to be fruitful and populate the earth. For the purpose of human companionship, He is told to procreate. As human beings made in the hands of one Creator, we are responsible for each other. Jesus Christ summarized our mutual responsibility beautifully in the following statement, "thou shalt love thy neighbor as thyself" (Matthew 22:39).

Further, the scripture adds another beautiful dimension to how man was made; God makes them male and female.

He blesses them, and gives both of them dominion over the earth and its creatures. So in this progression also we see God creating sexuality and instituting the marriage covenant for the human race:

> "And the LORD God said, it is not good that the man should be alone; I will make him an help meet for him.
>
> And the LORD God caused a deep sleep to fall upon Adam, and he slept: and he took one of his ribs, and closed up the flesh instead thereof;
>
> And the rib, which the LORD God had taken from man, made he a woman, and brought her unto the man. And Adam said, This is now bone of my bones, and flesh of my flesh: she shall be called Woman, because she was taken out of Man.
>
> Therefore shall a man leave his father and his mother, and shall cleave unto his wife: and they shall be one flesh" (Genesis 2:18, 21-24; cf. 1 Timothy 2:13).

Further still, we see the mystery of God's wisdom in having made them equal, He also makes them different. From the hands of the Creator, they are made equal, but different from each other; they are complimentary.

Today, there is a desperate attempt to redefine or define marriage, but marriage has been defined already for us by our Creator from the beginning. The metaphor of marriage is used as descriptive of the intimate relationship between Christ Jesus and His Church. Male and female belong to each other.

The first man was created adult male and adult female. The first male was called Adam and the first female was called Eve. Ever since God breathed the breath of lives into man, life has never ceased; there has always been an egg and a sperm. However these two alone don't produce life. There is always a divine oversight. Can we agree that if life is a prerogative of God, then, there is nothing like an illegitimate child even though a child born out of wedlock can be classified as a bastard? (Deuteronomy 23:2).

Man was told what to eat, a diet consisting of vegetables and fruits, man was permitted to eat meat only after the flood (Genesis 9:3). God prepared for them a lavished home called "the Garden of Eden," with the best of the best, and with all that man can ever dream; it was a home of abundance and overflow.

God also planted two trees in the midst of the Garden: the "tree of life," which man could freely eat and "the tree of knowledge of good and evil," from which he was specifically told not to eat. He was forbidden to eat of it. The consequence of disobedience was clearly spelled out to him, he will die:

"But of the tree of the knowledge of good and evil, thou shalt not eat of it: for in the day that thou eatest thereof thou shalt surely die" (Genesis 2:17).

Death has three segments: spiritual, physical, and eternal. Spiritual death is a temporal separation from the life of God and can be remedied. Physical death is cessation of breath or physical life; it is temporal and can be remedied. Eternal death is permanent separation from God and is irreversible; Spiritual death is the cause of both physical and eternal death. Man was warned by God not to eat of the tree of the knowledge of good and evil. The consequence for disobedience was death, meaning, all three forms of death will immediately happen to him (John 3:16-18; 11:25-26).

Probably a good question we may all ask is for whom was

this beautifully vast and complex planet made? Was it made
for man and for what purpose? The straight answer from the
Bible is, God created the universe for His pleasure:

> **"Thou art worthy, O Lord, to receive glory and hon-
> our and power: for thou hast created all things, and
> for thy pleasure they are and were created" (Revela-
> tion 4:11).**

The kingdoms, the powers, and the glories of this earth
belong to God: "For thine is the kingdom, and the power,
and the glory, forever. Amen. Again, God purposely made
every man, plant, and beast for His only Son, Jesus. As the
owner of the universe (Psalm 24:1), He gave the planet
earth to man as his habitation (Isaiah 45:18):

> **"For by him were all things created, that are in heav-
> en, and that are in earth, visible and invisible, wheth-
> er they be thrones, or dominions, or principalities, or
> powers: all things were created by him, and for him"
> (Colossians 1:16; cf. Psalm 50:10-12; 104).**

God is very active in history; not only does He sustain
the universe, but also protects it from being destroyed
prematurely by man. God is very much in control of the
affairs of this world. He is not a dead or absentee God and
neither is He an "I don't care kind of God." He loves and
cares very much for His world and the people on it.

When Jesus said He came to save that which was lost,
He was right on target. He made every one of us (Matthew
18:11); all was His from the beginning. Whether we like
it or not, we shall all one day appear before Him to render
account of our stewardship in the gifts, talents and time
spent in this life:

> **"For we shall all stand before the judgment seat of
> Christ" (Romans 14:10).**

Man as a recipient of God's benevolence has a duty to God. He is supposed to be thankful for all His blessings; worship Him with due reverence; love, obey and keep His commandments. This is the primary duty of man (Genesis 1:28; 2:16-17). Man is to love His maker unconditionally and to love his fellow man as himself (Ecclesiastes 12:13; Micah 6:8; 1John 3:23).

In conclusion, what was true of our parents, Adam and Eve, is also true for all of us. We were all in Adam when he was created in God's image and likeness so to speak. Man is God's masterpiece in creation, specially made with deliberation and counsel; he is like God in many ways without being equal to Him. He is a little world with God as his center. Man was upright as he came out from the hands of his Creator; he loved the Lord with all his soul and spirit. His body was a living sacrifice unto his maker. He was pure in spirit, soul and body (1 Thessalonians 5:23).

Beloved, there are no errors in the Bible; whatever God has said about us is infinitely true and must be accepted by all. Think about it, if not for what took place later, which is well explained in the next chapter, you and I will have been living a different kind of life. But let me say this, no matter what has happened to man and the world, there is plenty of hope. By the time you've finish reading this book, you will know with certainty that there is still much hope and good life ahead for each of us.

Chapter Two

THE FALL OF MAN

The fall of man was a dark day in the history of humanity. Never will the choice of any man surpass that which was made by Adam. The Bible does not give the exact date this incident took place, but from the Genesis account, it appears it was not long after man was made. Adam knowingly and deliberately chose to disobey. Adam and his wife Eve, parents of the human race, chose to belief the devil rather than take God at His word.

They broke a known command. Sin is the transgression of the Law (1John 3:4). They ate of the "tree of good and evil," the forbidden tree. They were free to eat of the "tree of life" and continue to live forever in a state of purity and fellowship with God, but they didn't. This is the Genesis account:

> "Now the serpent was more subtile than any beast of the field which the LORD God had made.
>
> And he said unto the woman, Yea, hath God said, ye shall not eat of every tree of the garden?
>
> And the woman said unto the serpent, we may eat of the fruit of the trees of the garden:

But of the fruit of the tree which is in the midst of the garden, God hath said, ye shall not eat of it, neither shall ye touch it, lest ye die.

And the serpent said unto the woman, ye shall not surely die:

For God doth know that in the day ye eat thereof, then your eyes shall be opened, and ye shall be as gods, knowing good and evil.

And when the woman saw that the tree was good for food, and that it was pleasant to the eyes, and a tree to be desired to make one wise, she took of the fruit thereof, and did eat, and gave also unto her husband with her; and he did eat" (Genesis 3:1-6).

Satan (also known as the Serpent, Devil, Lucifer, Tempter, Murderer, Father of lies, Destroyer, fallen angel), entered the Garden of Eden disguised in the body of the serpent. He first managed to deceive Eve to eat from the tree of 'knowledge of good and evil.' Eve then gave some to the husband who also ate. Adam, though fully aware of the command not to eat of the tree, willingly went along with his wife.

The Bible lays the fall of man squarely on Adam; "For Adam was first formed, then Eve. And Adam was not deceived, but the woman being deceived was in the transgression" (1Timothy 2:13). Adam, first to be created should have known better. His act was deliberate; his was a willful sin. He chose to disobey. He chose death instead of life and evil instead of good. His choice was for himself and his race; in other words, all those who will come after him.

At the heart of their disobedience, both wanted to be like God, to be self-governing. Both denied the will of God for their lives. They hated the divine imposition 'not to' eat. They wanted what pertains only to God, but chose disobedience as the means. Disobedience carries with it punishment; the soul that sinneth, it shall die (Ezekiel 18:4, 20).

Adam willingly abdicated his loyalty to God to follow his wife's ambition to be independent. In history, Adam is not alone in this heinous act; Herod and Ahab both followed the insane advice of their wives. They both preferred to be servants of Satan rather than God. They acted in open rebellion against the rule of God (Lamentations 1:18). Obedience to God is life everlasting:

"Know ye not, that to whom ye yield yourselves servants to obey, his servants ye are to whom ye obey; whether of sin unto death, or of obedience unto righteousness? (Romans 6:16).

Soon after eating the fruit their eyes were opened and both knew for the first time that they were naked. Sin ruins life and hope; they lost their covering. The potter's vessel, once adorned with holiness and glory, lies broken. Instead of wholeness they had brokenness. What they experienced can be referred to as 'I-chabod,' meaning the glory is departed from man (1Samuel 4:21). Man became spiritually and physically naked; he has lost his only covering — the garment of righteousness. There is no substitute for what they had lost. The universe cannot produce it; no factory can produce a copy. Only the Creator can provide such covering because it is His own kind of covering:

"And the eyes of them both were opened, and they knew that they were naked; and they sewed fig leaves together, and made themselves aprons" (Genesis 3:7).

Without this precious covering man is in every way unclean. His whole being has become corrupted; his soul is debased and body riddled with diseases and sicknesses.

His conscience is seared and blunted, his mind is vain, and will weakened. He is a slave to sin and Satan (Ephesians 2:2) and utterly lost (Luke 19:10). Sin defiles and corrupts the soul; without God's covering man is unclean. He is like snow trodden under foot or run over by trucks on an unpaved road.

Sin produces fear, failure, and disappointment. You gain nothing by sinning; instead, you lose everything. Sin produces separation; it separates man from God, man from man, and man from the rest of creation. Sin has seriously changed man's thought about himself and God; in place of love there is doubt, misunderstanding, and hatred. Sin has disrupted free access to God. The healthy and holy relationship between man and God was gone. Instead of friendship and togetherness, man has been running away from God ever since:

> "And they heard the voice of the LORD God walking in the garden in the cool of the day: and Adam and his wife hid themselves from the presence of the LORD God amongst the trees of the garden.
>
> And the LORD God called unto Adam, and said unto him, where art thou?
>
> And he said, I heard thy voice in the garden, and I was afraid, because I was naked; and I hid myself" (Genesis 3:8-10).

Man is unclean and needs a cleaner; he cannot make himself clean: "Who can bring a clean thing out of the unclean? No one" (Job 14:4). Fallen man does what is right in his own sight; if it made sense to him, then, it is right:

> "What is man, that he should be clean? And he which is born of a woman, that he should be righteous?

Behold, he putteth no trust in his saints; yea, the heavens are not clean in his sight. How much more abominable and filthy is man, which drinketh iniquity like water?" (Job 15:14-16).

Their punishment was swift and immediate. God, as usual, came down looking for them, but they were no where to be found. They had gone into hiding at the sound of His voice. When God demanded a reason for their action, both answered in self-rightness. Adam, setting his life at premium, blamed it on Eve and God. Eve blamed the serpent. Sin produces hardness of heart:

"And the man said, the woman whom thou gavest to be with me, she gave me of the tree, and I did eat.

And the LORD God said unto the woman, what is this that thou hast done? And the woman said, the serpent beguiled me, and I did eat" (Genesis 3:12-13).

However, God went ahead and pronounced their punishment in three statements. The fact that man was put under probation means temptation was permitted. Satan could only tempt and man must exercise his will. They had everything they need and will ever need in super abundance. God had made them rulers of the earth and it was their responsibility to guide and protect themselves and those under their stewardship from any intruder. They were forewarned:

To the serpent and Satan, the Lord God said:

"Because thou hast done this, thou art cursed above all cattle, and above every beast of the field; upon thy belly shalt thou go, and dust shalt thou eat all the days of thy life:

And I will put enmity between thee and the woman, and between thy seed and her seed; it shall bruise thy head, and thou shalt bruise his heel" (Genesis 3:14-15).

Pride goes before destruction (Proverbs 8:16). Satan himself once tried to be like God, but failed and was cast out of heaven. As if that was not evil enough, he came down to earth and managed through deceit to get the human race to rally behind him in his rebellion against God. Those of us who choose to be Satanist must read the Bible account of their master Satan. The meaning of his name 'Satan' is adversary or accuser (Ezekiel 28:11-19); he is the accuser of the brethren (Job 1:11).

Satan accused God of being jealous of His own superiority, and that His superiority would be threatened if they gain the knowledge hidden in the tree. But if what Satan said was true, then the question will be why will God create the very means of acquiring the knowledge that will undermine His own superiority? However, our parents, Adam and Eve believed the devil, and soon discovered their betrayal, Satan had lied. Sin is a lie and Satan is the father of lies. They were ensnared, deceived, and ruined. The purpose of Satan is to set our will against the will of God. He came to earth to steal, kill and destroy the soul of man (John 10:10).

Not withstanding, God promised that the seed of the woman (Jesus Christ), will destroy Satan's work; sin, death, and the damage done to humanity. However, it will be achieved at a great cost to Him, for Satan shall bruise His heel. The reference to the seed of the woman and not the man is the first Messianic promise: "Therefore the Lord himself shall give you a sign; Behold, a virgin shall conceive, and bear a son, and shall call his name Immanuel" (Isaiah 7:14). "But when the fullness of the time was come, God sent forth his Son, made of a woman, made under the law" (Galatians 4:4).

To the woman God said:

**"I will greatly multiply thy sorrow and thy concep-
tion; in sorrow thou shalt bring forth children; and
thy desire shall be to thy husband, and he shall rule
over thee" (Genesis 3:16).**

Her desire was to gain self-rule; instead, she was made
subject to her husband. In addition, she will experience pain
during childbirth. It appears the statement; "desire shall be
to thy husband" is reminiscent of Genesis 2:8 where the
function of the woman before the fall was spelled out (cf.
1 Timothy 2:9-15). Eve allowed her ears and eyes to feed
on the forbidden and her heart to run away with her desire.
Finally by her own free will, she committed the crime she
could readily have avoided.

To the man God said:

**"because thou hast hearkened unto the voice of thy
wife, and hast eaten of the tree, of which I commanded thee, saying, Thou shalt not eat of it: cursed
is the ground for thy sake; in sorrow shalt thou eat
of it all the days of thy life;**

**Thorns also and thistles shall it bring forth to thee;
and thou shalt eat the herb of the field;**

**In the sweat of thy face shalt thou eat bread, till
thou return unto the ground; for out of it wast thou
taken: for dust thou art, and unto dust shalt thou
return" (Genesis 3:17-19).**

Work for man shall no longer be enjoyable, satisfying,
and rewarding; instead, tilling the ground for food, clothing,
and shelter shall be drudgery, laborious, and vanity. Man
shall not live forever; the fruit of his hard work shall pass
on to another: "As he came forth of his mother's womb,

naked shall he return to go as he came, and shall take nothing of his labor, which he may carry away in his hand. And this also is a sore evil, that in all points as he came, so shall he go: and what profit hath he that hath labored for the wind?" (Ecclesiastes 5:15-16).

Man shall surely reap the wages of his sin, but due to the kindness and mercy of God, death was mitigated. God stopped the death sentence at physical death, and short of eternal death. This implied God had a plan to save man from eternal death. Even though man shall return to the dust of the earth, he might escape hell or eternal punishment (Revelation 21:8). Man will have another chance to decide destiny and choose whom to obey.

The surprising thing about the fall of man is that there is no indication Adam and his wife showed any remorse, admitted their fault, or even ask God for forgiveness for their crime against Him. It is amazing to see how their self-centeredness and self-righteousness has passed down the generations to us. After almost six thousand years, man is still in a state of denial and always finding ways for exoneration. He is full of self- rightness. Sin is a mistake that must be admitted and repented.

The Law of God is holy, spiritual, and good; it cannot be broken. Curse is everyone who breaks the Law of God (Romans 6:23; cf.7:12, 14, 16; 6:23; 1John 3:4). Sin entering the world became universal. Their sin brought evil on themselves and the race they represented; the existence of sin with all its attended sufferings is plain to all. Through Adam, the human race missed the mark; God's set standard for mankind. Man fell short of the glory of God. Today that standard is Jesus Christ. His righteousness is the standard for all men. There is only one race — the human race and all are descendants of Adam:

"Wherefore, as by one man sin entered into the world, and death by sin; and so death passed upon all men, for that all have sinned" (Romans 5:12):

"For all have sinned, and come short of the glory of God" (Romans 3:23).

Sin having entered the world through Adam found its dwelling place in the human heart and body. Not only did sin create disparity in the nature of man, but nature itself was also affected, for the ground was cursed. Today, Man and beast live in fear of each other and so is man with his neighbor, but in the beginning it was not so. Who knows, earthquakes, tornados, stormy winds, landslides, and all the upheavals in nature are the ramifications of sin?

Sin is ignorance of the ways of God. The light in them and around them was replaced with darkness (Matthew 6:23; John 3:19). The couple tried to cover their nakedness with fig leaves, another form of self-effort, independence, and rebellion. However, God is merciful; He dismissed their self-provided covering (self-righteousness), and re-clothed them temporarily with coats of skin until the Saviour comes:

". . . and they sewed fig leaves together, and made themselves aprons" (Genesis 3:7)

Sin has produced schism in man, faith in God is undermined with suspicion and mistrust; belief is replaced with disbelief. The heart of man is cold and self-centered. Man can only see himself. Sin, like a thick cloud, stands between fallen man and God. Instead of glory and innocence, there is shame and guilt (Isaiah 44:22). The heart of man is full of doubt and suspicion. Satan is constantly sowing the seed of doubt and unbelief in the heart of man.

Satan by questioning the integrity of God enticed Adam and Eve to rely on reason and logic to draw the conclusion to eat or not to eat of the forbidden tree. As expected, without faith as their guiding principle, reason and logic told them it was okay to eat of the tree:

"And when the woman saw that the tree was good for food, and that it was pleasant to the eyes, and a tree to be desired to make one wise, she took of the fruit thereof, and did eat, and gave also unto her husband with her; and he did eat" (Genesis 3:6).

True faith is demonstrated in love and obedience. Man's ground for existence is always threatened when faith is replaced with unbelief. The strength of man is his faith in God and there is no substitute for that (Matthew 4:4). The word of God is the foundation for faith; it is food for the soul and spirit and health for the body (Proverbs 4:22). When God goes everything goes, and the same applies to faith. Man is infinitely dependant upon His Creator for existence, sustenance, and happiness.

Reason, mind, and logic are great gifts from God. They are very useful, but unfortunately none of them can save or replace faith. Man was not created to operate by reason and logic alone, but on faith. Man with a finite mind must obey His infinite Creator who is Omniscience, Omnipotent, and Omnipresent. He must use his God-given capacity for thought, talents and other gifts to fulfill his God-given responsibilities. "Man is not to live by bread alone, (meaning what he can do for himself) but on every word that comes out of the mouth of the Lord," (Matthew 4:4).

Adam and Eve thought their decision to eat of the forbidden tree was the right thing to do, but it led them to death: "There is a way which seemeth right unto a man, but the end thereof are the ways of death" (Proverbs 14:12):

"Every way of a man is right in his own eyes: but the LORD pondereth the hearts" (Proverbs 21:2).

Many people believe God must understand them and not vice versa. The hypocrite says God must be content with some worship and must not demand too much; for them; God is even lucky to get their attention on Sundays and ten minutes every morning in prayer. The arrogant man says since he did not ask God to create him, He has no right to judge him. The religious man expects God to explain why he must judge him unrighteous if his unrighteousness commends His righteousness? The fool says there is no God.

Sadly, in the absence of faith in God, man has invented his own god, his own religion, and all kind of isms. In most cases, man has made himself the object of worship. To date, man still prefers self-government to the rule of God or theocracy. As already mentioned, Adam made the irreversible choice on behalf of us all. Legally, every unsaved person before the bar of God is guilty and under condemnation.

Fallen man is depraved and immoral. Even though we were not born as already said, when Adam committed the crime; not withstanding, we all have inherited the sinful and corrupt nature that became of them after the fall. The nature of man is ingrained with evil. His "mouth is full of cursing and bitterness" (Romans 3:14). We sin because we cannot, but sin; we are unable not to sin. You don't have to teach a child to lie; it comes naturally to all of us. "The wicked are estranged from the womb: they go astray as soon as they be born, speaking lies" (Psalm 58:3). We lie, cheat, steal, kill and hold the truth in unrighteousness:

"As it is written, there is none righteous, no, not one:

There is none that understandeth, there is none that seeketh after God.

They are all gone out of the way, they are together become unprofitable; there is none that doeth good, no, not one.

Their throat is an open sepulchre; with their tongues they have used deceit; the poison of asps is under their lips:

Whose mouth is full of cursing and bitterness:

Their feet are swift to shed blood:

Destruction and misery are in their ways:

And the way of peace have they not known: There is no fear of God before their eyes" (Romans 3:10-18; cf. Psalm 14:1-3).

We are labeled sinners not necessarily for sins committed, but because we are born that way, "Behold, I was shapen in iniquity; and in sin did my mother conceive me" (Psalm 51:5). Sin like leprosy has deformed the image and likeness of God in all men. Man is defaced beyond repair. The Bible looks at fallen man as dead in trespasses and sins (Ephesians 2:1). The only remedy is to be born again as Jesus told Necodemus (John 3). Rehabilitation won't restore him; man needs a transformation not a reformation. The damage caused by sin in man is beyond repair.

Marred by sin, man is imperfect in all his ways. He may be good, but also bad. The irrational and rational marks all his acts. Other than that, how do we explain all the madness around us; for example, the acts of a loving father who abuses his children or murders them? How do we explain the actions of a husband who murders his wife for a girlfriend? Can hate and love dwell in the same person?

The fall of man is our only rational answer to our current state of derailment, (the schism and disorientation in the nature of man); the presence of good and evil, and the meaninglessness of life. Man knows what is good, but won't or can't do it, rather, the evil he does not want to do is what he does. Man without the grace of God is not far from the wild beast of the forest. Paul bemoaned his own pathetic state which unfortunately is true for all of us without rebirth and the leading of the Spirit of God in the following statement:

> **"For to will is present with me; but how to perform that which is good I find not. For the good that I would I do not: but the evil which I would not, that I do.**
>
> **Now if I do that I would not, it is no more I that do it, but sin that dwelleth in me"**
>
> **I find then a law, that, when I would do good, evil is present with me.**
>
> **For I delight in the law of God after the inward man:**
>
> **But I see another law in my members, warring against the law of my mind, and bringing me into captivity to the law of sin which is in my members.**
>
> **O wretched man that I am! Who shall deliver me from the body of this death?"** (Romans 7:19-24).

The same hospital that saves life also kills the unborn child. The factories that produce planes to facilitate travel and enjoyment also produce the bomber plane that creates miseries and havoc. The same unit that provides energy through nuclear power also produces the atomic bomb that threatens to destroy the planet and everything on it. The government, chosen by the people and for the people, turns to deceive, maim, and in some cases kill them. Good and evil seems to co-exist and presents itself in all the works of mankind.

Sometimes I tremble when I think of how the unsaved will someday stand before the bar of a Just and holy God to account for his stewardship for the destruction of the rain forest, the sea, and the atmosphere which are the homes of the creatures he is mandated to care for (Romans 2:5-7). How will man defend himself on the judgment day before his maker with his hands stained with the blood of the innocent killed by wars and human greed?

Man denies his august creation in the hands of a good and holy God, but willing to accept his equality with the animals and even degrade further by accepting and believing in a creation by accident and chance, what a tragedy:

> "The fool hath said in his heart, there is no God. They are corrupt, they have done abominable works, there is none that doeth good.

> The LORD looked down from heaven upon the children of men, to see if there were any that did understand, and seek God.

> They are all gone aside, they are all together become filthy: there is none that doeth good, no, not one" (Psalm 14:1-3).

Yes, there may be some divine sparks and jewels in man as some people believe, but that does not negate the fact that man is perishing and needs help (Isaiah 64:6). This is not to say man is totally useless, but that man in his present composition of good and bad or depravity, is of no use to his Creator or himself. It is for all of the above reasons that man is said to be under the wrath of God. Man is not as his Creator made him. He cannot escape the consequences of his actions, he must die; he must suffer the full consequences of his actions. He must restore the broken relationship between him and his maker (1Corinthians 2:14).

The bad news for mankind is that man can't redeem himself. There is no way man can die to pay for his own sins and rise again from the dead to live a righteous life thereon before his maker. It is absolutely impossible for fallen man, who by nature hates God and at enmity with him, to negotiate peace and receive forgiveness.

However, there is also good news. God has stepped in to help mankind. He has provided a means for man to be restored through Jesus Christ. He came to earth because of the fall and its consequences. Jesus came to save us, to be the mediator, a ransom, man's substitute, and to die in man's place. He rose again from the dead to give man another opportunity to choose life and good.

God is just but also merciful. He was not willing to forsake His masterpiece, His handiwork, which is now marred with sin. His promise of the woman's seed destroying Satan and his work indicated a second chance. By His foreknowledge He knew what would become of man; a plan was already in place for his redemption. Man was and still is very dear to God.

Do not misconstrue the statement Jesus made when He said, "You belong to your father, the devil, and you want to carry out your father's desire. He was a murderer from the beginning, not holding to the truth, for there is no truth in him. When he lies, he speaks his native language, for he is a liar and the father of lies" (John 8:44).

Jesus did not mean God is no longer our Father by creation or that the devil gave birth to man. What He meant was, man in his current thought, words and deeds bears no resemblance to His Creator, the Holy God; instead, he is everything to do with the devil. He shares the same character with him; we possess his temper and his spirit.

Jesus came to redeem and to cleanse us from all rottenness and defilement. Fallen man has two problems; first, he is guilty and under condemnation before the bar of God. Secondly, he is a slave to sin; he is morally corrupt and perishing (Ephesians 2:1). God hates all the ungodliness and unrighteous acts of mankind; despite, He has paid in full what it takes to redeem us, and to restore us to our former glory. Each of us is given a second chance by God Himself to exercise the gift of the will, this time not against Him, but for Him; to choose life and good.

Finally, God made sure man does not seal his doom by eating from the tree of life. To give man another chance to change his circumstances, He drove Adam and Eve from the Garden. Man will have another chance some day to eat of the tree of life (Revelation 2:7; 22:2):

> **"So he drove out the man; and he placed at the east of the garden of Eden Cherubims, and a flaming sword which turned every way, to keep the way of the tree of life" (Genesis 3:24).**

Sin is what God says; it is not what society views as sin. If we fail to look at life in the mirror of God's word, we will have a low view of what our Saviour Jesus has done for humanity. Sometimes we think God is subject to change like us or the weather. For example, what was sin ten years ago is no more sin in our advanced and scientific age. We pick and choose what in our estimation constitutes sin.

God has already defined sin for us and will not accept any changes or accept man's definition. Almost the entire bible is devoted to sin, the ramifications of sin and the remedy for sin (or the restoration of fallen man). Sin is sin no matter how we camouflage it. Unless we agree with our maker's view of what has become of us and repent, we are doomed to perish.

In conclusion, I hope this chapter settles it once and for all the questions and doubts you may have had concerning the fall. What man needs is rebirth (John 3:3). He must be reborn; he must be born the second time by the Holy Spirit to resume fellowship with His Creator. To God be the glory for his mercy and kindness towards us and for not giving up on us, because in Christ Jesus, the curse of the fall is terminated (Galatians 3:28).

Chapter Three

THE HEART OF GOD

The heart of God aches for the return of His children. God, though just, is full of mercy, longsuffering and generosity. God has never given up on His estranged children. Ever since the fall of Adam, man has been running away from God, but He wants us to return to Him. The work of God at the moment is to reinstate man to his premier glory to be followed by the restoration of all things at a later date.

In the beginning, when God created all things, the Genesis account places man as the last to be created. However, in the restoration of all things, in the current work of God, man is being restored first or regenerated, and then nature itself would be restored. (Compare Genesis 1 with Romans 8:19-22).

God did not create us to die, but to live. It is His will and desire that we live and not die. He takes no delight or pleasure in the death of anyone, because that defeats the purpose for His creation. He is the God of the living and not of the dead. This does not also mean God will force people to accept His calling to repentance and live or bring about a universal salvation of all men as some teach, but rather, He desires that every man will be saved. Let us examine the heart of God from the following Scriptures:

> "Have I any pleasure at all that the wicked should die? saith the Lord GOD: and not that he should return from his ways, and live?" (Ezekiel 18:23; cf. 18:32; 33:11).

———————————

> "For this is good and acceptable in the sight of God our Savior; who will have all men to be saved and to come unto the knowledge of the truth" (1 Timothy 2:3-4).

———————————

> "For God so loved the world that he gave his only begotten Son, that whosoever believeth in him should not perish, but have everlasting life.

> For God sent not his Son into the world to condemn the world; but that the world through him might be saved" (John 3:16-17).

———————————

> "For the grace of God that bringeth salvation hath appeared to all men, teaching us that, denying ungodliness and worldly lusts, we should live soberly, righteously, and godly, in this present world" (Titus 2:11-12).

———————————

> "The Lord is not slack concerning his promise, as some men count slackness; but is longsuffering to us-ward, not willing that any should perish, but that all should come to repentance" (2 Peter 3:9).

The love of God cannot permit Him to forget His lost children by creation. He hates our sins, and our estrangement, but longs for our return. Jesus said His coming to earth was to seek and to save that which was lost. God created each man for a purpose and longs to see that purpose fulfilled.

Jesus revealed the heart of God and His longing for every one of His lost children in the parable of the lost Son. In this parable, God the Father of all mankind is set in the context of a father waiting and hoping for His estranged son to return to Him and to the home where everything is in profusion:

> And he said, "a certain man had two sons:
>
> And the younger of them said to his father, Father, give me the portion of goods that falleth to me. And he divided unto them his living.
>
> And not many days after the younger son gathered all together, and took his journey into a far country, and there wasted his substance with riotous living.
>
> And when he had spent all, there arose a mighty famine in that land; and he began to be in want.
>
> And he went and joined himself to a citizen of that country; and he sent him into his fields to feed swine.
>
> And he would fain have filled his belly with the husks that the swine did eat: and no man gave unto him.
>
> And when he came to himself, he said, How many hired servants of my father's have bread enough and to spare, and I perish with hunger!

I will arise and go to my father, and will say unto him, Father, I have sinned against heaven, and before thee,

And am no more worthy to be called thy son: make me as one of thy hired servants.

And he arose, and came to his father. But when he was yet a great way off, his father saw him, and had compassion, and ran, and fell on his neck, and kissed him.

And the son said unto him, Father, I have sinned against heaven, and in thy sight, and am no more worthy to be called thy son.

But the father said to his servants, Bring forth the best robe, and put it on him; and put a ring on his hand, and shoes on his feet:

And bring hither the fatted calf, and kill it; and let us eat, and be merry:

For this my son was dead, and is alive again; he was lost, and is found. And they began to be merry.

Now his elder son was in the field: and as he came and drew nigh to the house, he heard music and dancing.

And he called one of the servants, and asked what these things meant.

And he said unto him, Thy brother is come; and thy father hath killed the fatted calf, because he hath received him safe and sound.

And he was angry, and would not go in: therefore came his father out, and intreated him.

And he answering said to his father, Lo, these many years do I serve thee, neither transgressed I at any time thy commandment: and yet thou never gavest me a kid, that I might make merry with my friends:

But as soon as this thy son was come, which hath devoured thy living with harlots, thou hast killed for him the fatted calf.

And he said unto him, Son, thou art ever with me, and all that I have is thine.

It was meet that we should make merry, and be glad: for this thy brother was dead, and is alive again; and was lost, and is found" (Luke 15:11-32).

God is very concerned about the current state of man; He is concerned about His planet (Revelation 21). He hates the wickedness of mankind; for example, the killing of animals for sport and the indiscriminate destruction of their natural habitats. The duty of man is to protect and care for the animals and not to destroy them indiscriminately and for our entertainment.

God hates the classification of human beings into rich and poor, slave and master, etc. He created all men equal, and wants to see the dignity and respect of all men restored. He expects man to love his neighbor as himself. God cares for all including the so-called underdogs, slaves, strangers, and the poor. We ought to be very careful in the treatment of each other because God executes judgment for the oppressed:

"Which executeth judgment for the oppressed:

which giveth food to the hungry. The LORD looseth the prisoners:

The LORD openeth the eyes of the blind: the LORD raiseth them that are bowed down: the LORD loveth the righteous:

The LORD preserveth the strangers; he relieveth the fatherless and widow: but the way of the wicked he turneth upside down" (Psalm 7:-9).

His heart is forever inclusive; meaning, His heart goes out to each of us. Whether he chooses an individual, group or nation, His intention is always the same, that all may be blessed. There is no respect of persons with God (Romans 2:11):

"Every good gift and every perfect gift is from above, and cometh down from the Father of lights, with whom is no variableness, neither shadow of turning" (James 1:17).

Let me give you some examples: when God chose Noah to build the ark because of the judgment of flood which was to destroy the entire earth, it was not his plan to save Noah and his family only. He waited a very long time hoping that the people of Noah's days would repent of their wickedness and avoid the flood altogether (2Peter 2:5). It was rather unfortunate that with the exception of Noah and his family, the rest chose to continue in their ungodliness and unrighteousness and therefore perished:

"Which sometime were disobedient, when once the longsuffering of God waited in the days of Noah, while the ark was a preparing, wherein few, that is, eight souls were saved by water" (1Peter 3:20).

Even when the flood came, it was redemptive in nature; for God by His own grace saved eight souls from the family of Noah to allow the human race to continue, hoping that some of his offspring will follow the path of righteousness. Further, if not for the flood, you and I may not be alive today. We might have destroyed ourselves and the planet long ago by our own wickedness and madness. It is not the will of God that any man should perish.

Another example of the heart of God is in the story of Abraham. God called Him to vacate his home, family, and land to another place He would assign to him. God further said to Abraham: "in thee shall all the families of the earth be blessed" (Genesis 12:3). God promised to make out of Abraham a great nation, as part of his collateral blessings, but the primary purpose for the calling of this man was to be the channel through which the Seed promised to all mankind would come. Through his Seed (Jesus Christ) all the families of the earth shall be blessed:

> "That the blessing of Abraham might come on the Gentiles through Jesus Christ; that we might receive the promise of the Spirit through faith.
>
> Brethren, I speak after the manner of men; though it be but a man's covenant, yet if it be confirmed, no man disannulleth, or addeth thereto.
>
> Now to Abraham and his seed were the promises made. He saith not, And to seeds, as of many; but as of one, and to thy seed, which is Christ" (Galatians 3:14-16).

Further, the name Israel was the God-given name of the great grandson of Abraham. His original name was Jacob. Later this name was assigned to his twelve sons when they were officially formulated into a nation under the leadership of Moses. It is interesting to note all that time God was primarily dealing with the nation of Israel, He was simultaneously dealing with the rest of the

nations, sometimes passing judgment on them, other times
exonerating them:

> "Ye have seen what I did unto the Egyptians, and
> how I bare you on eagles' wings, and brought you
> unto myself.
>
> Now therefore, if ye will obey my voice indeed, and
> keep my covenant, then ye shall be a peculiar treasure
> unto me above all people: for all the earth is mine:
>
> And ye shall be unto me a kingdom of priests, and
> an holy nation. These are the words which thou shalt
> speak unto the children of Israel" (Exodus 19:4-6).

> "Are ye not as children of the Ethiopians unto me,
> O children of Israel? saith the LORD. Have not I
> brought up Israel out of the land of Egypt? and the
> Philistines from Caphtor, and the Syrians from
> Kir?" (Amos 9:7).

The primary purpose for the choice of Israel was to
be the extension of God's blessing to all mankind and to
be the instrument through which God will reveal His
Messiah, the Savior of the entire world.

Further still, the heart of God for all nations can be
seen in the calling of the twelve disciples by Jesus Christ.
He commanded them to go into all the nations starting
from Jerusalem to the uttermost ends of the world. They
were to preach the Gospel to every creature:

> "But ye shall receive power, after that the Holy
> Ghost is come upon you: and ye shall be witnesses
> unto me both in Jerusalem, and in all Judaea, and in
> Samaria, and unto the uttermost part of the earth"
> (Acts 1:8).

"Go ye therefore, and teach all nations, baptizing them in the name of the Father, and of the Son, and of the Holy Ghost:

Teaching them to observe all things whatsoever I have commanded you: and, lo, I am with you always, even unto the end of the world. Amen" (Matthew 28:19-20).

"And this gospel of the kingdom shall be preached in all the world for a witness unto all nations; and then shall the end come" (Matthew 24:14).

Apart from all that has been said, remember, man is a microcosm; he is a world by himself. His center is God. Even though man's nature is corrupted, he has other ways of acknowledging the existence and reality of God his Creator. I call them the signature of God. Even though they have no saving power, they are extremely helpful and important; they are conscience, reason and nature:

"For when the Gentiles, which have not the law, do by nature the things contained in the law, these, having not the law, are a law unto themselves" (Romans 2:14).

Conscience is a useful and great indicator. Even though seared and blunted, it is still very useful; it can alert you of wrong and right. Forever it stands to warn us of the existence of God and the impending consequences of our action. Conscience can be silenced, but can never be eradicated.

Man has an intuition or natural consciousness of God. Intuitively we are all in some way aware of the existence of God, even though some choose not to accept the fact. God is not far from any one of us; if we sincerely seek Him, we shall find Him:

"Because that which may be known of God is manifest in them; for God hath shewed it unto them" (Romans 1:19).

The physical universe is a monument of God's power and wisdom. Through the study of nature and its complexity and by deductive reasoning, man can come to some conclusion of the existence of the Creator:

"When I consider thy heavens, the work of thy fingers, the moon and the stars, which thou hast ordained. What is man, that thou art mindful of him? And the son of man, that thou visitest him?" (Psalm 8:3; cf. Psalm 19).

———————

"The heavens declare his righteousness, and all the people see his glory" (Psalm 97:6).

I guess we can all agree with the Psalmist that, "man is fearfully and wonderfully made" (Psalm 139). Man himself, his uniqueness, creativity and love, is a likeness to His Creator.

There is no way man can say there is no God; "For in Him we live, and move, and have our being" (Acts 17:28). The truth about God apart from His written word is also set within nature, so that man has no excuse. Those who brush God aside, those who try to remove God from their thoughts, and all those who say out of pride I have no need for God or time for God can consider themselves to be wicked people (Psalm 10:4; 14:1; 53:1):

"For the wrath of God is revealed from heaven against all ungodliness and unrighteousness of men, who hold the truth in unrighteousness;

because that which may be known of God is manifest in them; for God hath shewed it unto them.

For the invisible things of him from the creation of the world are clearly seen, being understood by the things that are made, even his eternal power and Godhead; so that they are without excuse" (Romans 1:18-20).

Again, one can see the kindness of God towards all in the given of the Law. Every nation has some form of ethical or moral laws to live by. The moral fiber in man though corrupted is not totally silenced. The law, be that of God, nation, tribe or self, though cannot bring salvation to any, may have some virtues to them; for example, they can in some cases reform. People for fear and the consequences of breaking the law may be refrained from certain acts.

Israel for example, had the Law of Moses which God delivered to them in a spectacular manner, but the main purpose was to awaken their consciousness of sin and to reveal their own inability to do that which was right in the sight of the holy God. Even though, the Law was not given for the purpose of salvation, it had redemptive benefits. Without the Law of God man would not have known fornication, lying, idolatry or adultery is a sin. The Law helps us to understand the nature of sin and our own helplessness so that we can run to God for grace and mercy:

"Therefore by the deeds of the law there shall no flesh be justified in his sight: for by the law is the knowledge of sin," (Romans 3:20).

"Wherefore then serveth the law? It was added because of transgressions, till the seed should come to whom the promise was made; and it was ordained by angels in the hand of a mediator" (Galatians 3:19).

To demonstrate the hardness and the wickedness in

the heart of man and how impossible it is for fallen man to obey His Law, God offered to grant eternal life to anyone who could fully obey them (Romans 5:14). Israel worked very hard, and offered many sacrifices and promises, despite, they all failed including Moses the agent of the Law. To date, with the exception of Jesus Christ, no man has and will ever fully obey the law of God:

> **"For there is no respect of persons with God. For as many as have sinned without law shall also perish without law: and as many as have sinned in the law shall be judged by the law"** (Romans 2:11-12).

The Mosaic Law was good and holy, but our flesh is weak and unable. Despite, the beauty and greatness of the Law could further be seen in the fact that it was our school master to bring us to Christ:

> **"But the scripture hath concluded all under sin that the promise by faith of Jesus Christ might be given to them that believe.**
>
> **But before faith came, we were kept under the law, shut up unto the faith which should afterwards be revealed.**
>
> **Wherefore the law was our schoolmaster to bring us unto Christ, that we might be justified by faith"** (Galatians 3:22-24).

> **"That they should seek the Lord, if haply they might feel after him, and find him, though he be not far from every one of us"** (Acts 17:27).

Above all the mentioned graces let me add the every day benevolences of our Good God. Reflect on your past, count your many blessings and you will be surprised how blessed you are. Problems and difficulties that could have crushed or killed you, but didn't. Times when you thought you were not going to make it, but for some unexplainable reasons you made it through. In many ways it may appear you are the lucky one among many, especially when you compare yourself with others in your family and peers. How many of your contemporaries are dead, sick or in some kind of trouble? Why not you and could it have been you?

It may be beneficial sometimes to slow down the fast lane lifestyle and reflect on the many blessings we take for granted. Like good health, good job, beautiful home, healthy children, wealth, and even beautiful and bright days. Can all these favors be channels through which God is drawing our attention to Himself? Stop and think, don't take them for granted. Can all these blessing be that God is calling on all to see His love for us, that we may by His longsuffering and kindness repent and return to Him?

The good news to all is that God is not any nation, tribe, or religious god; He is not a Christian guru. He is the Creator, sustainer, and redeemer of the universe. He is the Lord of all the earth; He is good and rich to all who call upon Him. His heart is warm toward each one of us and eager to get us saved. It is not His will that any of us perishes.

In the next chapter, you will see how the heart of God has provided grace for all through our Lord and Savior Jesus Christ and how the price of our salvation was fully paid for by God, and made free for all who will believe. The grace of God is personified in Christ Jesus and from Him all men can receive grace upon grace (John 1:16).

In conclusion, each of us, including you, is in God's plan. Grace is the ground on which God saves men, and by that all are included. Grace provides every one who is willing with a ticket to enter heaven. Beloved, the doors of heaven still stands open for you to enter. His heart reaches out to you.

Chapter Four

WHAT GOD HAS ALREADY DONE

God has fully fulfilled the promise He made to give man a second chance. "Her seed shall bruise thy head, and thou shalt bruise his heel" has been fulfilled. Almost two thousand years ago, God sent His only beloved Son into the world as He promised. Jesus Christ, seed of the woman, has already come and paid in full the price needed to free every one of us from the bondage and influence of sin, from the power of Satan and death, and to bestow upon us the lost glory:

"But when the fullness of the time was come, God sent forth his Son, made of a woman, made under the law" (Galatians 4:4).

"No man hath seen God at any time, the only begotten Son, which is in the bosom of the Father, he hath declared him" (John 1:18).

God has given the human race a savior, Jesus Christ. He is the full revelation of God to man and the only mediator between man and God:

"For this is good and acceptable in the sight of God our Savior;

Who will have all men to be saved, and to come unto the knowledge of the truth.

For there is one God, and one mediator between God and men, the man Christ Jesus; who gave himself a ransom for all, to be testified in due time" (1 Timothy 2:3-6).

God has done what He said He will do, He has done His part, it is now up to you and me to decide what to do with what has been done for us. Jesus paid for our offences with His own life. He gave His life a ransom for all (1 Timothy 2:6). The price he paid, He paid for every one in the world. God through Christ has paid for the sin and sins of the whole world. Through Christ the ransom, He has purchased the world and everything in it. The salvation of mankind was purchased not with silver and gold, but with the very life of the Son of God:

"Forasmuch as ye know that ye were not redeemed with corruptible things, as silver and gold, from your vain conversation received by tradition from your fathers;

But with the precious blood of Christ, as of a lamb without blemish and without spot" (1 Peter 1:18-19).

However, be aware that even though God has purchased us and the world through Christ, He can only plead with us to accept His generous offer; He will not force or do anything without our consent. His salvation is not universalism.

What God has done through His Son is awesome; it by far exceeds the crime committed by both Adam and Eve. God's overflowing grace for every man's salvation is that where sin abounds, grace much more abounds. No one is off limits. No matter what the nature of your sin there is room for you: "though your sins be as scarlet, they shall as white as snow; though they be red like crimson, they shall be as wool (Isaiah 1:18):

> "Wherefore, as by one man sin entered into the world, and death by sin; and so death passed upon all men, for that all have sinned:

> (For until the law sin was in the world: but sin is not imputed when there is no law.

> Nevertheless death reigned from Adam to Moses, even over them that had not sinned after the similitude of Adam's transgression, who is the figure of him that was to come.

> But not as the offence, so also is the free gift. For if through the offence of one many be dead, much more the grace of God, and the gift by grace, which is by one man, Jesus Christ, hath abounded unto many.

> And not as it was by one that sinned, so is the gift: for the judgment was by one to condemnation, but the free gift is of many offences unto justification.

> For if by one man's offence death reigned by one; much more they which receive abundance of grace and of the gift of righteousness shall reign in life by one, Jesus Christ.)

> Therefore as by the offence of one judgment came upon all men to condemnation; even so by the righteousness of one the free gift came upon all men unto justification of life.

For as by one man's disobedience many were made
sinners, so by the obedience of one shall many be
made righteous.

Moreover the law entered, that the offence might
abound. But where sin abounded, grace did much
more abound:

That as sin hath reigned unto death, even so might
grace reign through righteousness unto eternal life
by Jesus Christ our Lord" (Romans 5:12-21).

As quoted, by one man, sin entered the world and death
and condemnation by sin; and so death passed upon all
men, for all have sinned. By the offence of one man, death
and judgment came upon all men to condemnation; by one
man's disobedience many were made sinners. In the same
way, through the obedience and righteousness of one man
Jesus, righteousness and life comes to all who will believe:

"For as in Adam all die, even so in Christ shall all be
made alive" (1Corinthians 15:22).

Further, the one sin of Adam plunged the whole
of humanity into death, judgment, and condemnation;
likewise, by the one time sacrifice of the righteous man
Jesus Christ, many sins are covered. For example, I was
seventeen years of age when I was born again, and you
can just imagine how many sins I had already committed
against the Lord. But on that day, all (not just a few) of my
sins, were instantly washed away by the one-time vicarious
sacrifice of Christ on the cross when I believed. What a
great Salvation, a Salvation that has provision even for
future sins. Beloved reader, you are included in God's plan,
seize the opportunity while you can:

"But if we walk in the light, as he is in the light, we have fellowship one with another, and the blood of Jesus Christ his Son cleanseth us from all sin.

If we say that we have no sin, we deceive ourselves, and the truth is not in us. If we confess our sins, he is faithful and just to forgive us our sins, and to cleanse us from all unrighteousness" (1John 1:7-9).

Again, recounting on the overwhelming benefits of the sacrifice of Christ in contrast to the sin of Adam, this is what the Bible had to say:

"For since by man came death, by man came also the resurrection of the dead.

For as in Adam all die, even so in Christ shall all be made alive" (1Corinthians 15:21-22).

"And so it is written, the first man Adam was made a living soul; the last Adam was made a quickening spirit.

Howbeit that was not first which is spiritual, but that which is natural; and afterward that which is spiritual.

The first man is of the earth, earthy; the second man is the Lord from heaven.

As is the earthy, such are they also that are earthy: and as is the heavenly, such are they also that are heavenly.

And as we have borne the image of the earthy, we shall also bear the image of the heavenly" (1 Corinthians 15:45-49).

The generosity of God is overwhelming; in spite of the death brought about by the sin of Adam, He is willing to grant immunity from spiritual death to anyone simply by believing and accepting Jesus as Lord and Saviour. According to the Word of God, through many means and in diverse ways God spoke to our forefathers through the prophets, priests, kings, men and women, symbols and sacrifices and types, but now and finally, in these last days, He has spoken to us through His Son, Jesus Christ also known as the last Adam:

> **"God, who at sundry times and in divers manners spake in time past unto the fathers by the prophets, Hath in these last days spoken unto us by his Son, whom he hath appointed heir of all things, by whom also he made the worlds;**
>
> **Who being the brightness of his glory, and the express image of his person, and upholding all things by the word of his power, when he had by himself purged our sins, sat down on the right hand of the Majesty on high" (Hebrews 1:1-3).**

Jesus, as the final Word or message from God, may be hard for some to believe (probably including you), but it is the truth; it is absolutely impossible for God to lie. Many men, women, and founders of religions over the ages have laid claim to possessing divine powers. Many founders lay claim to having had divine callings from angels or having experienced some supernatural manifestations and revelations or divine callings to lead people into the light, immortality, or to God.

Many Jesus, messiahs, and prophets have come and gone, and many more are yet to come.

But, believe it or not, none can save their followers or even themselves from the bondage to sin and its ramifications. None of their writings can redeem man from sin and neither can they declare or make any man righteous before the Holy God. No man comes close to Jesus in His birth, works, teachings, death, resurrection, ascension, enthronement, and the continuous and powerful works done through His name by His disciples. He stands alone and above all men throughout history. Never shall the earth witness another man like Jesus Christ, the Son of the living God.

Jesus did not just claim to be a man, but also God. He left behind many infallible proofs of His deity. Witnesses heard voices from heaven; angelic beings testified of His deity, even demons testified of Him. On the morning of His resurrection, many saints also rose from the dead, all testifying to His deity. Jesus Christ is more than a man; He is God becoming man. He is the God-Man.

How comforting it is to know there is only one God; think about how confusing it would be if the United States, as one country, had fifty independent presidents. We must admit, Jesus being the only way and Savior is good for humanity. We don't have to search the whole universe looking for all the Saviors and many ways. There is only one God; He is not one God among many, but the one and only true God:

> "Ye are my witnesses, saith the LORD, and my servant whom I have chosen: that ye may know and believe me, and understand that I am he: before me there was no God formed, neither shall there be after me.
>
> I, even I, am the LORD; and beside me there is no savior" (Isaiah 43:10-11).

Jesus before He became man

John speaks of the existence of Jesus Christ beyond the beginning of the creation of all things. Before He came into the world, He is titled as the 'Word.' He is the Eternal Word:

"In the beginning was the Word, and the Word was with God, and the Word was God. The same was in the beginning with God" (John 1:1).

As the 'Word' He was in the beginning with God. He did not join God at a later date, and neither was He born by God. As the 'Word,' He was not inferior to God, but equal to God: "All things (universe) were made by Him; and without Him was not any thing made that was made" (John 1:3). He is the source of life to all men. He was part of the "Let us" in Genesis 1:26 and the "in-breathing" of man (Genesis 2:7). He is the light of men and the teacher of all who enter the world:

"And the Word was made flesh, and dwelt among us, (and we beheld his glory, the glory as of the only begotten of the Father,) full of grace and truth" (John 1:14).

"And the Word was made flesh;" That is the Word became man. The Word took upon Himself a human nature. Jesus is therefore presented to mankind as the 'Word become flesh.' In His incarnation He became identified with Adam's race. This is what God had to say about His Son Jesus when He sent Him to earth:

"Who is the image of the invisible God, the first-born of every creature:

For by him were all things created, that are in heaven, and that are in earth, visible and invisible, whether

they be thrones, or dominions, or principalities, or powers: all things were created by him, and for him:

And he is before all things, and by him all things consist.

And he is the head of the body, the church: who is the beginning, the firstborn from the dead; that in all things he might have the preeminence.

For it pleased the Father that in him should all fullness dwell;

And, having made peace through the blood of his cross, by him to reconcile all things unto himself; by him, I say, whether they be things in earth, or things in heaven.

And you, that were sometime alienated and enemies in your mind by wicked works, yet now hath he reconciled.

In the body of his flesh through death, to present you holy and unblameable and unreproveable in his sight" (Colossians 1:15-22).

This is what Jesus had to say about Himself while on earth. It was for the fact that He claimed to be God or the Son of God that the religious leaders of His day crucified Him (Luke 22:66-71; Mark 14:62-65):

"For as the Father hath life in himself; so hath he given to the Son to have life in himself" (John 5:26).

_____

"For the bread of God is he which cometh down from heaven, and giveth life unto the world" (John 6:33).

"Jesus said unto her, I am the resurrection, and the life: he that believeth in me, though he were dead, yet shall he live" (John 11:25).

"Then spake Jesus again unto them, saying, I am the light of the world: he that followeth me shall not walk in darkness, but shall have the light of life" (John 8:12).

"I am come a light into the world, that whosoever believeth on me should not abide in darkness" (John 12:46).

"And now, O Father, glorify thou me with thine own self with the glory which I had with thee before the world was" (John 17:5).

This is what His disciples who saw, touched, and ate with Him daily for over three years had to say:

"And we know that the Son of God is come, and hath given us an understanding, that we may know him that is true, and we are in him that is true, even in his Son Jesus Christ. This is the true God, and eternal life" (1John 5:20).

"That which was from the beginning, which we have heard, which we have seen with our eyes, which we have looked upon, and our hands have handled, of the Word of life;

(For the life was manifested, and we have seen it,

and bear witness, and shew unto you that eternal life, which was with the Father, and was manifested unto us" (1John 1:1-2).

_____

"For we have not followed cunningly devised fables, when we made known unto you the power and coming of our Lord Jesus Christ, but were eyewitnesses of his majesty" (2Peter 1:16).

_____

"And this is the record that God hath given to us eternal life, and this life is in his Son" (1John 5:11.

_____

"And killed the Prince of life, whom God hath raised from the dead; whereof we are witnesses" (Acts 3:15).

This also what the Apostle Paul had to say about Jesus the Christ:

"When Christ, who is our life, shall appear, then shall ye also appear with him in glory" (Colossians 3:4).

Why Jesus became man

Jesus became man because the people He had to redeem were men; they had a human nature, (not the angelic nature) and for that reason He also took upon Himself the human nature. He added to His divine nature our human nature:

"Forasmuch then as the children are partakers of

flesh and blood, he also himself likewise took part of the same; that through death he might destroy him that had the power of death, that is, the devil;

And deliver them who through fear of death were all their lifetime subject to bondage.

For verily he took not on him the nature of angels; but he took on him the seed of Abraham.

Wherefore in all things it behoved him to be made like unto his brethren, that he might be a merciful and faithful high priest in things pertaining to God, to make reconciliation for the sins of the people.

For in that he himself hath suffered being tempted, he is able to succour them that are tempted" (Hebrews 2:14-18).

God cannot die; it was therefore necessary if Jesus, the Son of God, had to taste death, or die for man, that He becomes man. Death for the Son of God was the only way to pay for the wages of sin, destroy Satan who had the power of death and restore relationship between God and man:

"Let this mind be in you, which was also in Christ Jesus:

Who, being in the form of God, thought it not robbery to be equal with God:

But made himself of no reputation, and took upon him the form of a servant, and was made in the likeness of men:

And being found in fashion as a man, he humbled

himself, and became obedient unto death, even the death of the cross.

Wherefore God also hath highly exalted him, and given him a name which is above every name:

That at the name of Jesus every knee should bow, of things in heaven, and things in earth, and things under the earth;

And that every tongue should confess that Jesus Christ is Lord, to the glory of God the Father" (Philippians 2:5-11).

Jesus dying for our sins broke the power of death; the sting of death is sin, and where there is no sin, Satan is powerless. Those who are made righteous by faith in Christ Jesus obtain eternal life; they shall not die but live. Satan having the power of death does not mean he created death, but that he introduced it into this world; he deceived man into choosing death rather than life. Jesus did not come to kill Satan or the devil (to take Satan and his demons out of existence); He came to destroy his work, to crush his power over man; to destroy the kingdom of Satan and to set up the kingdom of God:

"Jesus answered, My kingdom is not of this world: if my kingdom were of this world, then would my servants fight, that I should not be delivered to the Jews: but now is my kingdom not from hence.

Pilate therefore said unto him, Art thou a king then? Jesus answered; Thou sayest that I am a king. To this end was I born, and for this cause came I into the world, that I should bear witness unto the truth. Every one that is of the truth heareth my voice" (John 18:36-37).

Men throughout the ages for fear of death had invented many idols, gods, and engaged in various religious rituals for protection. Efforts to please the so-called gods have never been cheap; it has always been done at a great cost to the worshippers. Jesus came to set us free from the fear of death. Christians or believers need not therefore fear death. Jesus our brother has infinitely conquered death and Satan for us:

> **"Wherefore, holy brethren, partakers of the heavenly calling, consider the Apostle and High Priest of our profession, Christ Jesus"** (Hebrews 3:1).

To Abraham was promised, "through your seed (not seeds), all families of the earth would be blessed." It was therefore appropriate that the Messiah or Savior should come from the lineage of Abraham. Jesus died for both Jews and Gentiles. As already mentioned, Christ died to purchase the entire world (man, beast, plants, rivers, etc). He died to redeem all those who will believe in Him from sin and sin's power. He came to re-clothe fallen man with the righteousness of God and to offer them eternal life:

> **"Christ hath redeemed us from the curse of the law, being made a curse for us: for it is written, Cursed is every one that hangeth on a tree:**
>
> **That the blessing of Abraham might come on the Gentiles through Jesus Christ; that we might receive the promise of the Spirit through faith. . .**
>
> **Now to Abraham and his seed were the promises made. He saith not, And to seeds, as of many; but as of one, and to thy seed, which is Christ"** (Galatians 3:13-14, 16).

As a descendant of Abraham, he shared the same

ancestry with the physical and spiritual descendants of Abraham (Galatians 3:7); it was therefore proper that He called us brethren. He is compassionate and merciful to all, for He had a nature like our own and can relate to our feelings and pain. Coming into a world filled with violence, sin, sorrow and death, and having experienced the struggles of mankind against the tyranny of sin, He stands to sympathize with our sufferings:

> **"The LORD thy God will raise up unto thee a Prophet from the midst of thee, of thy brethren, like unto me; unto him ye shall hearken" (Deuteronomy 18:15).**

> **"Now of the things which we have spoken this is the sum: We have such an high priest, who is set on the right hand of the throne of the Majesty in the heavens" (Hebrews 8:1; cf. Hebrews 8 & 9).**

To my Jewish brethren, Jesus is that Prophet Moses spoke about to our forefathers in the wilderness "unto Him ye shall hearken." Jesus Christ, our current high Priest, replaces the Levitical High Priesthood of Aaron and Moses. His High Priesthood is of the order of Melchisedec (Hebrews 7), the man to whom Abraham paid tithe (Genesis 14:20).

As the High Priest, He makes reconciliation for the sins of all His people. Reconciliation was not necessary from God's side. Man has always been the offender; he is the one who has made God his enemy. For this reason, someone other than man has to step in to negotiate peace and reconciliation on man's behalf and this is where Jesus stands in as our High Priest. He won peace for us by offering Himself as the propitiation.

In Him the wrath of God was fully satisfied. There is,

therefore now peace between Man and God. He has also broken the middle wall that separated the people under the Old Covenant from the rest of the nations (Ephesians 2:14). Ascended into heaven and sitting on the throne, He guarantees the salvation of all who will believe:

> "My little children, these things write I unto you, that ye sin not. And if any man sin, we have an advocate with the Father, Jesus Christ the righteous: And he is the propitiation for our sins: and not for ours only, but also for the sins of the whole world" (1John 2:1-2; cf. Acts 20:28).

By the sacrifice of His own blood and life, he is able to cleanse us from sin and sins and to purify, and then present each of us to God without blemish:

> "Who gave himself for us, that he might redeem us from all iniquity, and purify unto himself a peculiar people, zealous of good works" (Titus 2:14).

Jesus died as our Substitute

The substitutionary work of Jesus Christ is the heart of the Gospel. There are serious charges against the human race, and for this reason Jesus came down from heaven to represent man. He came to provide a way out of the mess and to pay the ransom needed for our redemption. He died for all because all were dead in trespasses and sins without exception. Each of us can rightly say He died for me:

> "For when we were yet without strength, in due time Christ died for the ungodly. For scarcely for a righteous man will one die: yet peradventure for a good man some would even dare to die. But God com-

mendeth his love toward us, in that, while we were yet sinners, Christ died for us" (Romans 5:6).

_____

"For the love of Christ constraineth us; because we thus judge, that if one died for all, then were all dead:

And that he died for all, that they which live should not henceforth live unto themselves, but unto him which died for them, and rose again" (2 Corinthians 5:14-15).

God punished us in Christ. Jesus received the punishment that was due to us all. Even though He was without sin, God laid on Him the iniquities of us all:

"Surely he hath borne our griefs, and carried our sorrows: yet we did esteem him stricken, smitten of God, and afflicted.

But he was wounded for our transgressions; he was bruised for our iniquities: the chastisement of our peace was upon him; and with his stripes we are healed.

All we like sheep have gone astray; we have turned every one to his own way; and the LORD hath laid on him the iniquity of us all" (Isaiah 53:4-6).

He was sinless all the time He was on earth, never committed a single offense. He was spotless and blameless; yet, what should have befallen us fell upon Him. He suffered in our place:

"For Christ also hath once suffered for sins, the just for the unjust, that he might bring us to God, being put to death in the flesh, but quickened by the Spirit" (1Peter 3:18).

Because the Just suffered for the unjust, God is free
to credit His righteousness to any one who accepts Him
as his substitute. The atoning death of Christ validated
the justice of God; it gave God the freedom to forgive,
acquit and declare righteousness, and still be the just God.
Through Christ we can be what God wants us to be —
holy and righteous:

> "declare, I say, at this time his righteousness: that
> he might be just, and the justifier of him which be-
> lieveth in Jesus" (Romans 3:26).

He died for me, sums up all that Christ came to do.
Jesus tasted death for every man. Now you can understand
why you must be saved and why you must not go to hell.
Jesus died for you:

> "But we see Jesus, who was made a little lower than
> the angels for the suffering of death, crowned with
> glory and honor; that he by the grace of God should
> taste death for every man" (Hebrews 2:9).

Jesus died for all is very humbling; it eradicates all pride
and classifications among men. It levels all men before God.
The fact that one cannot actively contribute anything to his
salvation may be too much for some people to swallow, but
that is God's plan and not human works. Salvation is a gift
from God to each of us, fully paid for by Jesus Christ. His
coming was the beginning of a new order, and to prepare
a people for God. Jesus died and rose again to become the
representative of a new order. He is representative of all
those who will be made new:

> "But now is Christ risen from the dead, and become
> the firstfruits of them that slept" (1Corinthians
> 15:20).

The human race was under the curse of God for

breaking His Law. Instead, Jesus became a curse for us by His death on the cross; thus removing the curse, so that the blessing of God could freely flow to all who believe:

> "Christ hath redeemed us from the curse of the law, being made a curse for us: for it is written, Cursed is every one that hangeth on a tree.

> That the blessing of Abraham might come on the Gentiles through Jesus Christ; that we might receive the promise of the Spirit through faith" (Galatians 3:13-14).

We become identified with Him in His death by accepting Him as our savior. Those who receive Jesus as Lord and Savior are considered crucified with Him and resurrected with Him; they resurrect to a whole newness of life:

> "I am crucified with Christ: nevertheless I live; yet not I, but Christ liveth in me: and the life which I now live in the flesh I live by the faith of the Son of God, who loved me, and gave himself for me" (Galatians 2:20).

Let me give you some biblical examples to clarify this very important chapter. Take the Old Testament way of expiating sins for example. On the Day of Atonement, the great day the sins of the Nation of Israel were expiated, two goats are presented before the Lord, and Aaron is to cast lot upon the two goats; one goat for the Lord and the other lot as a scapegoat. The goat for the Lord is killed and its blood carried within the veil and sprinkled once upon the Mercy-Seat and seven times before it. The scapegoat is presented alive before the Lord, and the sins of the people confessed over it by the High Priest and let go into the wilderness.

This ceremony portrays the two main aspects of Christ's death; He makes peace with His own blood in the heavenly Tabernacle of which that of Moses was only a shadow. He is also the sin bearer, the dumping place of the sinner's sins. Jesus is the Lamb of God who takes away the sins of the world which is represented in the case of the scapegoat (Leviticus 16):

"Behold the Lamb of God, which taketh away the sin of the world" (John 1:29).

Further, Aaron had to take the blood of the sacrificial goat to atone for his own sin and that of the nation. Jesus, had no sin of His own to atone, He offered His own blood instead of the blood of animals for us. His sacrifice was a one-time offering and needed no repetition like the Aaronic sacrifices. God accepted His sacrifice as sufficient for all time, all ages and for all men. Never again will animal sacrifice be accepted by God to expiate sin. The blood of goat and sheep could only atone for the people of Israel externally and was therefore limited, but that of Jesus is for all mankind externally and internally:

"But Christ being come an high priest of good things to come, by a greater and more perfect tabernacle, not made with hands, that is to say, not of this building;

Neither by the blood of goats and calves, but by his own blood he entered in once into the holy place, having obtained eternal redemption for us.

For if the blood of bulls and of goats, and the ashes of an heifer sprinkling the unclean, sanctifieth to the purifying of the flesh:

How much more shall the blood of Christ, who through the eternal Spirit offered himself without

spot to God, purge your conscience from dead works to serve the living God?" (Hebrews 9:11-14).

The Old Testament sacrifices were only a shadow of the better things to come in Christ Jesus (Colossians 2:17). Animal and human sacrifices, libations, curious arts, shapes and numbers and all kinds of rituals are abominations in the sight of God. Those of us who engage in ritualistic forms of worship as a means of placating sins or pleasing God must stop or else we shall be found to be enemies of God instead. Let us do what the early believers in Christ did by saving the time and money for good works:

"And many that believed came, and confessed, and shewed their deeds.

Many of them also which used curious arts brought their books together, and burned them before all men: and they counted the price of them, and found it fifty thousand pieces of silver" (Acts 19:18-19).

All the Old Testament Covenants, Laws, Sacrifices and Ceremonies have their fulfillment in the person of Christ Jesus. Not that God has cancelled them, but that they have done their job, they have been fulfilled and therefore laid to rest in Christ Jesus:

"For the law having a shadow of good things to come, and not the very image of the things, can never with those sacrifices which they offered year by year continually make the comers thereunto perfect.

For then would they not have ceased to be offered? Because that the worshippers once purged should have had no more conscience of sins.

But in those sacrifices there is a remembrance again made of sins every year.

For it is not possible that the blood of bulls and of goats should take away sins.

Wherefore when he cometh into the world, he saith, Sacrifice and offering thou wouldest not, but a body hast thou prepared me:

In burnt offerings and sacrifices for sin thou hast had no pleasure.

Then said I, Lo, I come (in the volume of the book it is written of me,) to do thy will, O God.

Above when he said, Sacrifice and offering and burnt offerings and offering for sin thou wouldest not, neither hadst pleasure therein; which are offered by the law;

Then said he, Lo, I come to do thy will, O God. He taketh away the first that he may establish the second.

By the which will we are sanctified through the offering of the body of Jesus Christ once for all" (Hebrews 10:1-10; cf. Colossians 2:17).

Christ was our substitute while on earth; He was our substitute while on the cross and still our substitute in heaven. I can gladly say He was our substitute even before He became a man. He was our substitute before the world was made (Romans 4:21). Even now in heaven, He is the advocate of all believers:

"Who verily was foreordained before the foundation of the world, but was manifest in these last times for you, Who by him do believe in God, that raised him

up from the dead, and gave him glory; that your faith and hope might be in God" (1 Peter 1:21).

Another great example of the substitutionary work of Christ is that of Abraham and his son Isaac on Mount Moriah. At God's command Isaac was bound and placed upon an altar Abraham had built for the purpose. Abraham, with knife raised, ready to slaughter his son, was halted by an angel of the Lord. He was told to use a ram caught by the horns in the thicket. Abraham offered the ram instead of his son Isaac. We can see Christ as the ram caught by the horns in the thicket. Again, we can see Christ in Isaac, who was obedient even to the point of death (Genesis 22). Isaac the beloved son of Abraham was not sacrificed, but Jesus the beloved and only Son of God was sacrificed for each of us.

Jesus came down from heaven purposely to be our substitution. He came to live, die, and rise again on our behalf. He willingly offered Himself for us all. His was voluntary; He gave Himself voluntarily. God did not force Him to be our substitute; He did it because of His own love for us. He offered to take our sin and sins upon Himself so that we could be free to serve God in holiness and with a pure conscience. He came that we might have life and have it more abundantly. He came to seek for that which was Lost; a lost humanity:

"And he is the propitiation for our sins: and not for ours only, but also for the sins of the whole world" (1John 2:2).

God set forth Christ as the all-sufficient propitiation. He is the one who propitiates and offers Himself as the propitiation. He is the Savior of the world (John 4:42):

"And we have seen and do testify that the Father sent the Son to be the Savior of the world" (1John 4:14).

The wrath against Adam and the rest of humanity was satisfied in our substitute. Not only did His death break a peace deal for us, but He Himself became our peace. Believers through Him can approach God with boldness and not in fear. Believers can approach God as a loving Father without guilt and the threat of punishment from an angry Holy God:

> "For God hath not appointed us to wrath, but to obtain salvation by our Lord Jesus Christ,
>
> who died for us, that, whether we wake or sleep, we should live together with him.
>
> Wherefore comfort yourselves together, and edify one another, even as also ye do" (1 Thessalonians 5:9-11).

> "For the love of Christ constraineth us; because we thus judge, that if one died for all, then were all dead:
>
> And that he died for all, that they which live should not henceforth live unto themselves, but unto him which died for them, and rose again. . .
>
> For he hath made him to be sin for us, who knew no sin; that we might be made the righteousness of God in him" (2 Corinthians 5:14-15, 21).

The death of Jesus removed the barrier that stood among men, for example between Jews and Gentiles, male and female, literate and illiterate, rich and poor, slave and free (Galatians 3:28; Colossians 3:11). No human classifications can qualify any man before the holy God; they are of no use to Him. The cross of Jesus is a leveler; all must come to the cross if all are to be saved. Adam's sin was judged at the cross and done away with forever. Positionally, I mean before God, Adam's race has become a thing of the past.

All those who put their faith in Jesus Christ are considered dead with Him and if He rose to a new life, then, all believers will also rise to a new life. "As He is, so are we," or so we will be. Because He lives, we shall also live (John 14:19):

> "Therefore if any man be in Christ, he is a new creature: old things are passed away; behold all things are become new" (2 Corinthians 5:17).

> He "was delivered for our offences, and was raised again for our justification" (Romans 4:25).

Because of what Jesus has done for all mankind, God has committed to every believer the ministry of reconciliation, which is to preach the Gospel of Christ to every one; and this is the message we preach, "God has punished humanity in His Son; He has laid on Him the iniquity of us all." As a result, He is inviting and pleading with each of us to accept His offer and live. Why should you die and perish? (2 Corinthians 5: 18-20). And again, for this purpose, this book was written:

> "Blessed is the man unto whom the LORD imputeth not iniquity, and in whose spirit there is no guile" (Psalm 32:2).

The one and only sin that can condemn any one to hell is the rejection of Jesus Christ as Savior and Lord. The will of God is that each of us be saved (2 Timothy 4:1):

> "For God sent not his Son into the world to condemn the world; but that the world through him might be saved.

He that believeth on him is not condemned: but he that believeth not is condemned already, because he hath not believed in the name of the only begotten Son of God" (John 3:17-18).

In conclusion, Jesus died for all; Jews and Gentiles, poor and the rich, educated and uneducated, slaves and masters, and most importantly you. If you were the only sinner on the face of the earth, still Jesus would have come to die for you; this is how much God loves and cares about you. You are not just a number, a Buddhist, Islam, Bahaullah, Krishna, black or white etc. (none of these matters).

The most important is that, Jesus died for you. God loves you enough to make His only Son to die for you. You are precious in the eyes of your maker. Jesus is not a Christian god or guru, martyr, good man, prophet or perfect man; He is God who became man to die for you.

No more Sacrifice

In view of all that had been said about Jesus Christ and the Sacrifice made for our Salvation, it is clear we may be choosing our own condemnation if we remain skeptic and unbelieving. If we refuse to surrender our lives to Him, we shall surely be in danger of hell fire:

> "How shall we escape, if we neglect so great salvation; which at the first began to be spoken by the Lord, and was confirmed unto us by them that heard him;
>
> God also bearing them witness, both with signs and wonders, and with divers miracles, and gifts of the Holy Ghost, according to his own will?" (Hebrews 2:3-4).

If we continue in the vain conversations received by the tradition of our fathers, rituals and old women fable, and be spoiled by vain philosophy and deceit, after the tradition of men, after the rudiments of this world, and not after Christ (Colossians 2:8), we may have ourselves to blame. In Jesus we are complete. There is no more sacrifice after Christ Jesus:

"And ye are complete in him, which is the head of all principality and power" (Colossians 2:10).

There is no more sacrifice for sin; He is the final sacrifice, the only hope of all men. Only Jesus can save man from sin. In fact, Jesus on several occasions warned us to take heed that no man deceives us:

"And Jesus answered and said unto them, Take heed that no man deceive you.

For many shall come in my name, saying, I am Christ; and shall deceive many.

And ye shall hear of wars and rumors of wars: see that ye be not troubled: for all these things must come to pass, but the end is not yet.

For nation shall rise against nation, and kingdom against kingdom: and there shall be famines, and pestilences, and earthquakes, in divers places.

All these are the beginning of sorrows.

Then shall they deliver you up to be afflicted, and shall kill you: and ye shall be hated of all nations for my name's sake.

And then shall many be offended, and shall betray one another, and shall hate one another.

And many false prophets shall rise, and shall deceive many.

And because iniquity shall abound, the love of many shall wax cold.

But he that shall endure unto the end, the same shall be saved.

And this gospel of the kingdom shall be preached in all the world for a witness unto all nations; and then shall the end come...

For there shall arise false Christs, and false prophets, and shall shew great signs and wonders; insomuch that, if it were possible, they shall deceive the very elect" (Matthew 24:4-14, 24).

Paul the Apostle also warned Christians to beware of false doctrines; teachings that has its source from man and not God:

"That we henceforth be no more children, tossed to and fro, and carried about with every wind of doctrine, by the sleight of men, and cunning craftiness, whereby they lie in wait to deceive;

But speaking the truth in love, may grow up into him in all things, which is the head, even Christ" (Ephesians 4:14-15).

To add my own admonitions let us not be wise in our own eyes, but trust in the wisdom of God. We should let God be God; let us take Him at His word:

"Let no man deceive himself. If any man among you seemeth to be wise in this world, let him become a fool, that he may be wise.

For the wisdom of this world is foolishness with God. For it is written, He taketh the wise in their own craftiness.

And again, The Lord knoweth the thoughts of the wise, that they are vain" (1 Corinthians 3:18-20).

———————

"Be ye therefore followers of God, as dear children;

And walk in love, as Christ also hath loved us, and hath given himself for us an offering and a sacrifice to God for a sweetsmelling savor.

But fornication, and all uncleanness, or covetousness, let it not be once named among you, as becometh saints;

Neither filthiness, nor foolish talking, nor jesting, which are not convenient: but rather giving of thanks.

For this ye know, that no whoremonger, nor unclean person, nor covetous man, who is an idolater, hath any inheritance in the kingdom of Christ and of God.

Let no man deceive you with vain words: for because of these things cometh the wrath of God upon the children of disobedience.

Be not ye therefore partakers with them" (Ephesians 5:1-7).

Beloved, there is no Salvation in any human being save Jesus Christ:

"Neither is there salvation in any other: for there is

none other name under heaven given among men, whereby we must be saved" (Acts 4:12).

There is only one God and between man and God, the man Christ Jesus:

"For there is one God, and one mediator between God and men, the man Christ Jesus;

who gave himself a ransom for all, to be testified in due time" (1 Timothy 2:5-6).

To deny Jesus is to deny God. Apart from Jesus no man has seen God in His essence. He is the only one who can make God known to us because He is God and lives with God and He is God:

"Who is a liar but he that denieth that Jesus is the Christ? He is antichrist that denieth the Father and the Son.

Whosoever denieth the Son, the same hath not the Father: he that acknowledgeth the Son hath the Father also" (1 John 2:22-23).

———————

"And this is the record, that God hath given to us eternal life, and this life is in his Son.

He that hath the Son hath life; and he that hath not the Son of God hath not life" (1 John 5:11-12).

———————

"All things are delivered unto me of my Father: and no man knoweth the Son, but the Father; neither knoweth any man the Father, save the Son, and he to whomsoever the Son will reveal him" (Matthew 11:27).

God has highly exalted the name of His Son Jesus, so that He could be everything for each of us. Believers can use His name as a password for all that they need including destroying the powers of the devils. Take for example, demons screamed at the mention of His name, dead men came back to life, and diseases of all kinds were healed by the power of His name:

> "And the seventy returned again with joy, saying, Lord, even the devils are subject unto us through thy name" (Luke 10:17).

> "And whatsoever ye shall ask in my name, that will I do, that the Father may be glorified in the Son. If ye shall ask any thing in my name, I will do it John" (14:13-14).

> "Wherefore God also hath highly exalted him, and given him a name which is above every name:
>
> That at the name of Jesus every knee should bow, of things in heaven, and things in earth, and things under the earth;
>
> And that every tongue should confess that Jesus Christ is Lord, to the glory of God the Father" (Philippians 2:9-11).

God has raised His Son from the dead and sat Him at His own right hand in the heavenly places for us. He has made Him Lord and Christ for us:

> "Which he wrought in Christ, when he raised him from the dead, and set him at his own right hand in the heavenly places,

Far above all principality, and power, and might, and dominion, and every name that is named, not only in this world, but also in that which is to come" (Ephesians 1:20-21; cf. Acts 2:36).

Let me quote Peter's sermon on the day of Pentecost, and his testimony concerning Jesus before the Jewish leaders and all those who had gathered from all over the world:

"And it shall come to pass, that whosoever shall call on the name of the Lord shall be saved.

Ye men of Israel, hear these words; Jesus of Nazareth, a man approved of God among you by miracles and wonders and signs, which God did by him in the midst of you, as ye yourselves also know:

Him, being delivered by the determinate counsel and foreknowledge of God, ye have taken, and by wicked hands have crucified and slain:

Whom God hath raised up, having loosed the pains of death: because it was not possible that he should be holden of it.

For David speaketh concerning him, I foresaw the Lord always before my face, for he is on my right hand, that I should not be moved:

Therefore did my heart rejoice, and my tongue was glad; moreover also my flesh shall rest in hope:

Because thou wilt not leave my soul in hell, neither wilt thou suffer thine Holy One to see corruption.

Thou hast made known to me the ways of life; thou shalt make me full of joy with thy countenance.

Men and brethren let me freely speak unto you of the patriarch David that he is both dead and buried, and his sepulchre is with us unto this day.

Therefore being a prophet, and knowing that God had sworn with an oath to him, that of the fruit of his loins, according to the flesh, he would raise up Christ to sit on his throne;

He seeing this before spake of the resurrection of Christ, that his soul was not left in hell, neither his flesh did see corruption.

This Jesus hath God raised up, whereof we all are witnesses.

Therefore being by the right hand of God exalted, and having received of the Father the promise of the Holy Ghost, he hath shed forth this, which ye now see and hear.

For David is not ascended into the heavens: but he saith himself, The Lord said unto my Lord, Sit thou on my right hand,

Until I make thy foes thy footstool.

Therefore let all the house of Israel know assuredly, that God hath made the same Jesus, whom ye have crucified, both Lord and Christ.

Now when they heard this, they were pricked in their heart, and said unto Peter and to the rest of the apostles, Men and brethren, what shall we do?

Then Peter said unto them, Repent, and be baptized every one of you in the name of Jesus Christ for the

remission of sins, and ye shall receive the gift of the Holy Ghost" (Acts 2:21-38).

The whole book of Acts is dedicated to what the name of Jesus did for the early believers and what He can do for us. The disciples of Jesus did wonders using His exalted name and so can we. John concluded his Gospel on this note:

"And there are also many other things which Jesus did, the which, if they should be written every one, I suppose that even the world itself could not contain the books that should be written. Amen" (John 21:25).

Let me be very clear on this truth again; Jesus' death was and is for every man. But that does not mean God is granting spiritual amnesty to every man in the world. Every one of us willingly chose death in Adam; likewise, each of us must also willingly choose life in Christ Jesus. The two men stand for death or life for every one of us. What God has done through His Son Jesus Christ will benefit only those who acknowledge His invitation to accept His Son as their Lord and Personal Savior. The death of Jesus is not universalism; we must all will our Salvation or damnation.

Where to spend eternity is solely up to us; it is a personal responsibility. You must make this decision now, while you have the chance; procrastination is a thief of the soul. No one knows what may happen tomorrow? Today may be your last chance, so seize the moment. God is willing to forgive present, past, and future sins.

For all those who will not accept his last invitation to be reconciled to Him, His wrath and indignation remains. But those who acknowledge and accept their poor state and seek for salvation and immortality by the faith of His Son, they would be granted grace, mercy, and acceptance. This is His warning, "Woe unto him that striveth with his maker, shall the clay say to him that fashioned it, what maketh thou?" (cf. Isaiah 45:9).

In conclusion, it is ok to accept what Jesus has done and achieved on your behalf. It is ok to accept His invitation to put your faith in Him and be reconciled to Him; it is your reasonable duty and the right thing to do. You can't postpone your destiny.

The most important decision in your life is now before you. Faith in Jesus will deliver you from the wrath to come (1 Thessalonians 1:10). Your spiritual correctness must supersede your other ambitions in life. What is your life without God; it is vanity. Think of this parable as told by the Lord Jesus:

> "The kingdom of heaven is like unto a certain king, which made a marriage for his son.
>
> And sent forth his servants to call them that were bidden to the wedding: and they would not come.
>
> Again, he sent forth other servants, saying, Tell them which are bidden, Behold, I have prepared my dinner: my oxen and my fatlings are killed, and all things are ready: come unto the marriage.
>
> But they made light of it, and went their ways, one to his farm, and another to his merchandise:
>
> And the remnant took his servants, and entreated them spitefully, and slew them. But when the king heard thereof, he was wroth: and he sent forth his armies, and destroyed those murderers, and burned up their city.
>
> Then saith he to his servants, the wedding is ready, but they which were bidden were not worthy.

Go ye therefore into the highways, and as many as ye
shall find, bid to the marriage.

So those servants went out into the highways, and
gathered together all as many as they found, both
bad and good: and the wedding was furnished with
guests" (Matthew 22:2-10).

Righteousness Provided

This is the better part of the cake so to speak; Through
Jesus, God has made available to each of us His kind
of righteousness. This kind cannot be found in nature,
the world, religion, idolatry, and not even in the Law as
delivered to Moses. It can only be found in Jesus. He is
God's righteousness for all, and available to all who will
come to Him by the faith of Jesus. It is free for all fully paid
for by the blood of Jesus. The righteousness which God
provides is not a thing but a person, the person of Christ
Jesus:

"For he hath made him to be sin for us, who knew
no sin; that we might be made the righteousness of
God in him" (2Corinthians 5:21).

"Who his own self bare our sins in his own body on
the tree, that we, being dead to sins, should live unto
righteousness: by whose stripes ye were healed"
(1Peter 2:24).

God made Jesus sin not a sinner; God imputed our sin
to His spotless Lamb Jesus, so that He could impute His
righteousness to us who believe. By faith, He laid down
His life for us, trusting in God, who alone is able to raise

Him back to life. By His faith, He was willing to suffer the shame and the reproach of the Cross:

"But of him are ye in Christ Jesus, who of God is made unto us wisdom, and righteousness, and sanctification, and redemption" (1Corinthians 1:30; cf. 1Corinthians 1:24).

What Jesus is to God, He has made Him same to us. God loves every believer just the same way as He loves Jesus His beloved. The same Jesus who is the wisdom and power of God has been made unto us wisdom, righteousness, sanctification, and redemption (1Corinthians 1:30). The Lord God is our righteousness and the covering of His people (Jeremiah 23:6).

Righteousness belongs to the Lord; only God can credit and impart righteousness. They that fear the name of God and seek His protection shall the sun of righteousness arise with healing in His wings (Malachi 4:2). Those who hunger and thirst after righteousness shall be filled (Matthew 5:6).

Any one who is in Christ Jesus is set for life here and hereafter (Colossians 2:10). The righteousness which God provides never fades or need improvement; you can never become less holy or overly holy. It is never earned; you can't work for it or merit. It can only be imputed or credited. It is given as a gift by grace through faith to all who express the need and come to God by Christ. The Spirit of God will only live and work in the vessel that is declared righteous by God:

"Even as David also describeth the blessedness of the man, unto whom God imputeth righteousness without works" Romans 4:6.

"For if by one man's offence death reigned by one; much more they which receive abundance of grace

and of the gift of righteousness shall reign in life by one, Jesus Christ" (Romans 5:17; cf. verse 21).

The righteousness of God is by faith and faith alone. Gentiles and Jews alike must come to God by Faith to receive (Romans 9:30). In Christ Jesus, truth and mercy meet; righteousness and peace kiss each other (Psalm 85:10). Righteousness and judgment are the habitation of His throne (Psalm 94:15). He is the righteous branch:

"Christ is the end of the Law for righteousness to every one that believeth" (Romans 10:4).

In Christ the Law of God is laid to rest, it is no longer obligatory to Salvation, but the spontaneous result of Salvation. Jesus came to fulfill the Law of God and this He did. No man, apart from Christ Jesus, has ever fully obeyed the law of God, Moses, Abraham and David, were all declared righteous by their faith in God (Romans 4:1-12). They were all saved by grace and not by their obedience to the Law:

"Therefore by the deeds of the law there shall no flesh be justified in his sight: for by the law is the knowledge of sin" (Romans 3:20; cf. 4:13-24).

If righteousness could be achieved by the efforts of man or obedience to the Mosaic Law, there would have been no need for grace and faith through Jesus:

"I do not frustrate the grace of God: for if righteousness come by the law, then Christ is dead in vain" (Galatians 2:21).

The righteousness which God alone provides can only be found in the Gospel. The Gospel is the answer for righteousness. The word of God gives faith through grace to every seeking sinner:

"For therein is the righteousness of God revealed

from faith to faith: as it is written, the just shall live by faith" (Romans 1:17).

Even though this righteousness is not based on the Law, it is witnessed by the Law and the Prophets (Romans 3:21). Under grace the Law is replaced by the Spirit of God. If we live in the Spirit and He lives in us, the Law of God is fulfilled in us:

"For what the law could not do, in that it was weak through the flesh, God sending his own Son in the likeness of sinful flesh, and for sin, condemned sin in the flesh:

That the righteousness of the law might be fulfilled in us, who walk not after the flesh, but after the Spirit" (Romans 8:3-4; cf. 2Corinthians 3-4).

In the death of Jesus the believer also died to the law, thus becoming judicially free to be married to another — Jesus:

"Wherefore, my brethren, ye also are become dead to the law by the body of Christ; that ye should be married to another, even to him who is raised from the dead, that we should bring forth fruit unto God" (Romans 7:4).

Sin levels all men before the Holy God; therefore, all must come trusting to be saved by faith through grace alone. All must come depending on the mercy of God (Romans 11:15). The Law was our schoolmaster to bring us to Christ so that we might be justified by faith (Galatians 3:24, 26). After faith came, the job of the schoolmaster was no more needed.

I am not saying that the unsaved cannot do good works. Unbelievers throughout the centuries have pioneered all

kinds of social services and still do, and we must be grateful
for that. Unfortunately, the good works a man does cannot
save him on the Day of Judgment. We must receive the
righteousness God provides before our good deeds can
count for us.

When we come to God as undeserving guilty sinners,
we are immediately granted pardon, acquittal, and
proclaimed righteous. A court of law can pardon a guilty
felon, but can never pronounce him righteous (meaning
he never committed any offence), that will be injustice.
However, God by virtue of what Christ has done on our
behalf, a guilty helpless sinner asking for mercy through
Jesus can be declared righteous — no charge (no indication
of offence committed, records are clean):

> **"There is therefore now no condemnation to them
> which are in Christ Jesus, who walk not after the
> flesh, but after the Spirit . . .**
>
> **Who shall lay any thing to the charge of God's
> elect? It is God that justifieth. Who is he that con-
> demneth?**
>
> **It is Christ that died, yea rather, that is risen again,
> who is even at the right hand of God, who also ma-
> keth intercession for us"** (Romans 8:1, 33-34).

As already mentioned, Adam, during the fall lost God's
righteous covering, he tried to cover himself with his own
works, but God took it off and replaced it with something
temporary till the Seed comes. Jesus by His death provided
the final and acceptable covering for man; the covering of
His own glory. Man through Him can be reconciled to
God and on this note all men are invited!

To drive home the issue on righteousness, let us look
at the parable of the wedding banquet as foretold by Jesus.

Those originally invited refused to come, therefore, an invitation was sent out to 'whosoever will' to come. Many from all walks of life came including the poor, halt, lame, rich, bad and good, moral and immoral, etc., and the place was parked full.

Every one who came was issued wedding garments fit for the occasion (robes of righteousness in the case of God). However, when the king came to inspect his quest, he found one person without a wedding garment and this is what followed;

> "And when the king came in to see the guests, he saw there a man which had not on a wedding garment:
>
> And he saith unto him, Friend, how camest thou in hither not having a wedding garment? And he was speechless.
>
> Then said the king to the servants, Bind him hand and foot, and take him away and cast him into outer darkness, there shall be weeping and gnashing of teeth.
>
> For many are called, but few are chosen" (Matthew 22:11-14).

Whereas in this parable the man without the wedding garment was able to get in, no one without the garment of righteousness will enter or see the Kingdom of God. We cannot expect God to accept our own standard of righteousness when we reject what He has provided. This does not negate the fact that one cannot manufacture his own righteousness, yes we can, but that will be self-righteousness and unprofitable. Man-made righteousness is only right and acceptable to man, but not God:

> "But we are all as an unclean thing, and all our righteousnesses are as filthy rags; and we all do fade as a

leaf; and our iniquities, like the wind, have taken us away" (Isaiah 64:6).

In the sight of God, what man may exalt and claim to be good and right may be filthy rags. Only ignorant men waste time and effort to create their own moral standard:

"For they being ignorant of God's righteousness, and going about to establish their own righteousness, have not submitted themselves unto the righteousness of God" (Romans 10:3).

"What is man, that he should be clean? And he which is born of a woman, that he should be righteous?

Behold, he putteth no trust in his saints; yea, the heavens are not clean in his sight.

How much more abominable and filthy is man, which drinketh iniquity like water?" (Job 15:14-16).

If we compare ourselves one with another we fall in danger of declaring ourselves righteous. We can only get a true assessment of ourselves if we use the word of God or Jesus as the standard. It is absolutely impossible for man to live a life consistent to the nature of God by his own effort:

"For there is not a just man upon earth, that doeth good, and sinneth not" (Ecclesiastes 7:20).

In conclusion, the righteousness of God is the starting place for any dealings between God and men. Without it, the door is forever shut to all men. Righteousness provided is the only way and it is free to all men. It is a gift from God through Christ to all men. The grace of God makes it possible to all sinners who see their need for God and are hungry and thirsty for righteousness to receive. Be ready to receive, God is waiting for you.

Chapter Five

FROM FAITH TO FAITH

Faith to faith is how righteousness is obtained; how the righteousness of Jesus is imputed or credited to us; and how it becomes a personal possession. It is the process by which a sinner becomes a Child of God; sins forgiven, declared righteous, and heaven bound and many more. The quality of the two faiths is the same:

> **"For therein is the righteousness of God revealed from faith to faith: as it is written, The just shall live by faith"** (Romans 1:17).

The righteousness which God alone can provide is transmitted from faith through faith to faith. It is faith from beginning to finish. New life in Christ makes no room for works of the flesh or human efforts; it is a life of faith, and a life lived in the Holy Spirit. "The just shall live by faith (Habakkuk 2:4). Two faiths are required of anyone who wants to receive the righteousness of God. The two faiths are the faith of Jesus Christ Himself and the faith of the one needing salvation or the sinner seeking to be born again:

"Even the righteousness of God which is by faith of Jesus Christ unto all and upon all them that believe: for there is no difference" (Romans 3:22).

"But the scripture hath concluded all under sin, that the promise by faith of Jesus Christ might be given to them that believe" (Galatians 3:22).

The faith of Jesus is His own faith in God; His total trust and obedience to the word of God while He was on earth. As a man, he had to believe God to grant power to overcome evil, work miracles and have His daily needs met. He died for our offences and was raised for our justification by His personal faith. His resurrection abolished death, making it of no effect by His own faith in God. In fact, all that Jesus accomplished for us all were done through His personal faith in God; His total trusts in the word of God. His faith is not transferable, but all He did can be credited or imputed.

The other faith is what we must have in order to be saved. Faith comes to every one who hears the Gospel of Jesus Christ. The Gospel is the faith or the answer to faith. Faith through the Gospel is released by the Holy Spirit through grace. All that Jesus did will benefit no one unless each of us believes like He did:

"For I am not ashamed of the gospel of Christ: for it is the power of God unto salvation to every one that believeth; to the Jew first, and also to the Greek" (Romans 1:16).

Every believer is given 'the measure of faith,' or some faith which then becomes a personal faith (Mark 5:34; Acts 3:16; Romans 12:3; Ephesians 4:7). It is God's gift to all who hear the Gospel of His Son. It is God's response to all who thirst and hunger after righteousness. Both faiths rely 100% on God:

"So then faith cometh by hearing, and hearing by the word of God" (Romans 10:17).

Personal faith or Gospel provided faith cannot be earned or merited; it can only be given, and is free for all. It is the God-kind of faith; it is the faith that only God has, and can provide. This God-kind of faith, "calleth those things which be not as though they were" (Romans 4:17). It can move mountains, execute the will of God on earth and make impossible things possible (Matthew 18:18-19). It creates the New Man, and makes it possible for the everlasting God to tabernacle in believers.

By this same faith the Old Testaments saints did wonders in the name of God; whole armies fled when no man chased them; great rivers parted in two creating dry roads for the people of God to pass through; raging storms were silenced, and loved ones had their dead raised back to life. This God-kind of faith does not contradict reasoning but transcends. It does not question the integrity of His maker. Its achievements also transcend that of reasoning, and goes where reasoning dare not tread. It is not an abstract belief in the wisdom of men; neither is it the intelligent acts of the mind.

For example, Adam and Eve had their reasoning intact, yet, relying on that alone led them and the whole of mankind into the mess we find ourselves today. Reasoning and science are good, but unfortunately, they cannot fully explain God, or give an answer to how man can be saved. It has no room for sin and the Son of God who died on the cross for humanity. The cross of Jesus becomes unexplainable, if not foolishness in the face of science and reason.

God transcends human reasoning. For example, if God had not introduced Himself to mankind, there was no way man could have known His Creator. The ways of God are passed finding; He is able to do exceeding abundantly above all that we ask or think (Ephesians 3:20):

"For my thoughts are not your thoughts, neither are your ways my ways, saith the LORD" (Isaiah 55:8).

The good thing about faith is that it receives all from God and gives all to God without questioning. "Thy faith has saved thee" is true for everyone that believes (Luke 7:50). It did for Abraham, and it will do for you (Romans 4:22-25). "Thy faith has made you whole, go in peace," is also true for all who will believe the good news of the Gospel of Jesus Christ (Mark 5:34). Remember, "Without faith it is impossible to please God," (Hebrews 11:6) and this applies to every human being:

"But to him that worketh not, but believeth on him that justifieth the ungodly, his faith is counted for righteousness" (Romans 4:5).

Jesus died for the whole world is true, unfortunately, that alone cannot save anyone without a corresponding faith. Anyone in need of salvation or the righteousness of God, must have personal faith in the finished work of Christ to benefit thereof. We must all with no exception, believe the Gospel. His atonement is not universalism; we must ratify His faith with our faith to make it our own. So great a Salvation, cannot be forced on anyone; God respects the will of every man (John 7:17).

It cannot be that Jesus should be the only one to believe or love and obey the commandments of God. We too must believe, love, and obey. True faith is demonstrated in love and obedience to the commandment of God (1John 2:3). The faith of Jesus must be matched with our own faith for

Him to be our substitute and be credited with all that He accomplished on man's behalf.

Since God initiated Salvation, and offered His Son as a ransom for all, man must be given the opportunity to accept or reject His offer. It won't be right for God to load it on man. We must all be allowed to use the gift of free will to decide our destiny and this is exactly what God has done. All are invited but each of us must either accept or reject. If all are to benefit from the finished work of God's only Son, then all must believe. To believe is to give full credit to, or trust in His substitutionary work. Believe and faith can be used interchangeably.

Faith is the foundation stone of Salvation; it is the substance of things hoped for, the evidence of things not seen. No one can be saved without personal faith in God; neither can any man live successfully the Christian faith without continuous or abiding faith in God (Hebrews 11). The Apostle Paul hit the nail on the head when he said he lives his daily life by the faith of Jesus:

> **"I am crucified with Christ: nevertheless I live; yet not I, but Christ liveth in me: and the life which I now live in the flesh I live by the faith of the Son of God, who loved me, and gave himself for me" (Galatians 2:20).**

There is righteousness imputed and reckoned to us judicially through the all-sufficient propitiation of Christ on the cross when we believe in Jesus. His standing before God is forever righteous; His credit is forever good and able to off-set any spiritual bankruptcy. When our faith joins that of Christ, it ratifies what He did for us. All that He earned become ours or credited to us. God declares us righteous, accepts and loves us with the same love that He has for His Son Jesus.

Simultaneously, there is righteousness imparted — there is righteousness wrought in us by the Holy Spirit. Instantly, the Holy Spirit miraculously provides us with a new heart, a new spirit, washes us clean and makes His home in us. Both imputation and impartation are instant and complete. The result of regeneration is the new Man (born Again or new creature). Not only are you born by the Spirit, but also indwelt by the Spirit.

The Spirit then releases power for practical daily holy living. Our standing before God changes from sinner to saint; from guilt to righteous; from condemnation to justified, and all because of what happened on the cross. The cross is where the love, the wrath of God, the sins of mankind, and wages of sin clashed; and the outcome was peace towards men. Faith to faith forms an everlasting bond or union between the Son of God and any one who is born again. Jesus becomes our wisdom, righteousness, sanctification, and redemption (1Corinthians 1:30). We become one with the Son of God. He becomes our elder brother:

> **"For both he that sanctifieth and they who are sanctified are all of one: for which cause he is not ashamed to call them brethren" (Hebrews 2:11).**

Because of Him our sins are forgiven (1John 2:12). We receive eternal life; and pass from death into life, from the kingdom of Satan to that of God and His Son. We become children of God and therefore joint heirs with Christ. God becomes our Father. In fact, Apostle Paul describes the new standing in Christ beautifully in the following statements:

> **"And you hath he quickened, who were dead in trespasses and sins;**
>
> **Wherein in time past ye walked according to the**

course of this world, according to the prince of the power of the air, the spirit that now worketh in the children of disobedience:

Among whom also we all had our conversation in times past in the lusts of our flesh, fulfilling the desires of the flesh and of the mind; and were by nature the children of wrath, even as others.

But God, who is rich in mercy, for his great love wherewith he loved us,

Even when we were dead in sins, hath quickened us together with Christ, (by grace ye are saved;)

And hath raised us up together, and made us sit together in heavenly places in Christ Jesus:

That in the ages to come he might shew the exceeding riches of his grace in his kindness toward us through Christ Jesus.

For by grace are ye saved through faith; and that not of yourselves: it is the gift of God:

Not of works, lest any man should boast.

For we are his workmanship, created in Christ Jesus unto good works, which God hath before ordained that we should walk in them" (Ephesians 2:1-10).

Every time God looks at His Son, He sees us together with Him. He is the head; we are His body. He is the groom; we are His bride. Union with Christ is what makes heaven a reality. Union provides the saint access by the Holy Spirit to the heavenly Father. Joy and peace are the fruit of the union.

"In whom we have boldness and access with confidence by the faith of him" (Ephesians 3:12).

Faith can be seen as the tube through which all the graces of God in Christ flow. His faith is what sustains and keeps us perpetually holy before the Holy God. He is our guarantee to heaven. Faith to faith releases power to overcome all the trials and temptations in life. Our union with Him gives us grace to be successful in all things. We become more than conquerors. However, our faith must forever remain connected to His faith for all that to happen. The power to accomplish comes to all through our faith in the power of His name:

> **"Who shall separate us from the love of Christ? Shall tribulation, or distress, or persecution, or famine, or nakedness, or peril, or sword?**
>
> **As it is written, for thy sake we are killed all the day long; we are accounted as sheep for the slaughter.**
>
> **Nay, in all these things we are more than conquerors through him that loved us.**
>
> **For I am persuaded, that neither death, nor life, nor angels, nor principalities, nor powers, nor things present, nor things to come,**
>
> **Nor height, nor depth, nor any other creature, shall be able to separate us from the love of God, which is in Christ Jesus our Lord" (Romans 8:35-39).**

Without Him we can do nothing; however, with Him all things are possible. We must trust the faith of Jesus to save us, to sustain us, and bring us to glory in His presence. We must believe to be saved and keep believing to be glorified. We must hold fast to all His accomplishments for us, and stand on them to defeat the enemy and win. No man can manufacture his own faith; self-made faith is not faith at all, it has everything to do with self-righteousness:

> "Here is the patience of the saints: here are they that keep the commandments of God and the faith of Jesus" (Revelation 14:12).

What to do

Now, this is what you must do. I believe at this stage you are ready and cannot wait to be born of God; you have the faith. What kept you reading this book is faith. You are not far from the Kingdom of God. You are ready to join your faith with his; to make all His accomplishment yours. Beloved, the good news is, Jesus is not far away, and He is already knocking on the door of your heart, ready to come in:

> "Behold, I stand at the door, and knock: if any man hear my voice, and open the door, I will come in to him, and will sup with him, and he with me" (Revelation 3:20):

The words to say and how to say it is already in your heart and mouth:

> "But what saith it? The word is nigh thee, even in thy mouth, and in thy heart: that is, the word of faith, which we preach;
>
> That if thou shalt confess with thy mouth the Lord Jesus, and shalt believe in thine heart that God hath raised him from the dead, thou shalt be saved.

For with the heart man believeth unto righteousness; and with the mouth confession is made unto salvation.

For the scripture saith, whosoever believeth on him shall not be ashamed.

For there is no difference between the Jew and the Greek: for the same Lord over all is rich unto all that call upon him.

For whosoever shall call upon the name of the Lord shall be saved" (Romans 10:8-13).

According to the scripture just read, you must do two things. First believe with all your heart that Jesus died for you and that God raised Him from the dead. This you have done by your readiness and desire to be saved. You could have thrown this book away and have nothing to do with it, but you didn't. The second and last thing to do is to confess with your mouth, 'Jesus is Lord (owner, master). Since you believe with your heart, let it come out of your mouth, say it: "we have the same spirit of faith, according as it is written, I believed, and therefore have I spoken; we also believe, and therefore speak" (2Corinthians 4:13).

Just to help you, say this prayer; ratify His finished substitutionary work with your faith by praying the following:

"Lord Jesus I believe you died for me, I believe you rose from the dead for me, I accept you Jesus as my Lord and personal savior. Come into my heart and forgive me all my sins. Thank you Lord, for saving me" Amen.

That is it, beloved you are saved, born again, sanctified,

a Christian, child of God, new creature, etc. You have made it into the kingdom of God. Is that simple? Yes. The complicated and expensive part has already been done for you by God in Christ Jesus, who is now your Lord. Begin to call and acknowledge your newness. Your cry is answered. There should be no more fears and no more doubts.

Maybe you felt something; shaken, trembling, eyes swollen with tears, some relief, the feeling of a heavy load lifted, etc, or maybe you felt nothing — that is ok and perfect. Your Salvation is not based on feelings, but facts, on the word of God. The promises of God are ye and Amen. It is absolutely impossible for God to lie:

"And this is the record that God hath given to us eternal life, and this life is in his Son.

He that hath the Son hath life; and he that hath not the Son of God hath not life" (1John 5:11-12).

You will not die, but live. Jesus Christ is at the moment living in your heart by His Holy Spirit. You are therefore in Christ and Christ is in you; Christ is in God and God is in Christ and so you are in God by Christ Jesus. God the Father, Son, and Holy Spirit are all with you and in you. Wherever one is, the others are in the shadows. You are blessed from this moment. Your name is confirmed in the book of life. Now, go ahead and fill in your spiritual birth certificate:

Certificate of Spiritual Birth

Name:_____

Date of spiritual birth: _____

Time of spiritual birth:_____

Place: _____

Signature: The Lord Jesus Christ.

Water Baptism

Now that you are a Christian or born again, the next thing to do is to get baptized with water. Jesus commanded all His followers to be baptized. Baptize (Greek baptize) is an English translation, and means to "dip," "plunge under water," or "immerse," indicating its proper mode:

"And Jesus came and spake unto them, saying, all power is given unto me in heaven and in earth.

Go ye therefore, and teach all nations, baptizing them in the name of the Father, and of the Son, and of the Holy Ghost" (Matthew 28:18-19).

Baptism is the external or outward expression of what has taken place inwardly (inside you). It is the profession of your faith. It is the means of identification with the body of Christ. Because you are a Christian you must be baptized and this should always be the case and not vice versa. It is a command and not an option. It speaks to the world (meaning friends, family, etc.) of your union with Jesus Christ and with the Father. It signifies you are buried with Him and resurrected together by grace through faith to a new individual.

> **"Know ye not, that so many of us as were baptized into Jesus Christ were baptized into his death?**
>
> **Therefore we are buried with him by baptism into death: that like as Christ was raised up from the dead by the glory of the Father, even so we also should walk in newness of life"** (Romans 6:3-4).

Baptism is your public declaration of faith in God and union with His Son Jesus Christ. Sometimes obedience to this act can be very costly. In some extreme cases of religious hatred, it could cost you your life or bring you great hardship; you may lose some very dear friends or even parental love. But remember, no matter how grievous or painful our suffering may be, it cannot be compared with the sufferings of our Saviour. He suffered even to the point of death on a shameful cross. Baptism is your unashamed public testimony of your union with Him; meaning, you are the reason for His shame.

> **"For as many of you as have been baptized into Christ have put on Christ"** (Galatians 3:27).

In the face of persecution always remember what Jesus Said:

> **"Whosoever therefore shall be ashamed of me and of my words in this adulterous and sinful generation; of him also shall the Son of man be ashamed, when he cometh in the glory of his Father with the holy angels"** (Mark 8:38).

If you know of any pastor, minister, or a local church that believes in water Baptism ask if they can baptize you, let them know you had been saved or a Christian in need

of Baptism. If you can't get any Church or minister to
do it, any mature Christian who is baptized in water by
a Bible believing Church can do it for you. Ask the Holy
Spirit who now resides in you to help you in your search.
If you find a local Bible believing Church it may help to
fellowship with them.

A swimming pool, river, the sea or any safe and clean body
of water will do. The procedure is simple: First, pray together,
thank God together for your new found faith in Jesus. Ask
Jesus together to officiate the ceremony for you. Sit or squat
in the water; depending on the nature of the water, be sure
you have a decent cloth to cover any nakedness.

Let the Christian Brother or Sister put one hand on
your head and the other enclosing your two hands and then
dip you under the water and immediately bring you up
while saying "I baptize you in the Name of the Father, the
Son and the Holy Spirit." Amen. If you need a baptismal
certificate, then, have a recognized religious body do the
Baptism. They will then issue you a baptismal certificate.

Some churches or local congregation use only the
name 'Jesus' in water Baptism. Using the name Jesus alone
appears to be a practice going back to the days of the
Apostles e.g. in Samaria (Acts 8:16). However, this usage
does not eliminate the express command of the Lord to
baptize using the personal names of the Godhead. The
apostles were strict adherent of the teachings of Jesus
and would no way abdicate such an express command (2
Corinthians 13:14):

> 'Now when the apostles which were at Jerusalem
> heard that Samaria had received the word of God,
> they sent unto them Peter and John:
>
> Who, when they were come down, prayed for them,
> that they might receive the Holy Ghost:

> (For as yet he was fallen upon none of them: only they were baptized in the name of the Lord Jesus" (Acts 8:14-16; cf. 2:38; cf. 10:47-48).

Baptism was practiced by the early disciples:

> "Then Peter said unto them, Repent, and be baptized every one of you in the name of Jesus Christ for the remission of sins, and ye shall receive the gift of the Holy Ghost.
>
> Then they that gladly received his word were baptized: and the same day there were added unto them about three thousand souls" (Acts 2:38; cf. Acts 2:41; 8:12-13, 36, 38; 9:18; 10:47-48; 16:15, 33; 18:8; 22:16).

Here is a sample of Baptism by water:

> "And the angel of the Lord spake unto Philip, saying, Arise, and go toward the south unto the way that goeth down from Jerusalem unto Gaza, which is desert.
>
> And he arose and went: and, behold, a man of Ethiopia, an eunuch of great authority under Candace queen of the Ethiopians, who had the charge of all her treasure, and had come to Jerusalem for to worship,
>
> Was returning, and sitting in his chariot read Esaias the prophet.
>
> Then the Spirit said unto Philip, Go near, and join thyself to this chariot.
>
> And Philip ran thither to him, and heard him read the prophet Esaias, and said, Understandest thou what thou readest?

And he said, How can I, except some man should guide me? And he desired Philip that he would come up and sit with him.

The place of the scripture which he read was this, He was led as a sheep to the slaughter; and like a lamb dumb before his shearer, so opened he not his mouth:

In his humiliation his judgment was taken away: and who shall declare his generation? for his life is taken from the earth.

And the eunuch answered Philip, and said, I pray thee, of whom speaketh the prophet this? of himself, or of some other man? Then Philip opened his mouth, and began at the same scripture, and preached unto him Jesus.

And as they went on their way, they came unto a certain water: and the eunuch said, See, here is water; what doth hinder me to be baptized?

And Philip said, If thou believest with all thine heart, thou mayest. And he answered and said, I believe that Jesus Christ is the Son of God.

And he commanded the chariot to stand still: and they went down both into the water, both Philip and the eunuch; and he baptized him.

And when they were come up out of the water, the Spirit of the Lord caught away Philip, that the eunuch saw him no more: and he went on his way rejoicing.

But Philip was found at Azotus: and passing through he preached in all the cities, till he came to Caesarea" (Acts 8:26-42).

In conclusion, through baptism you have demonstrated that you are truly dead to the old life and resurrection to a new life in Christ Jesus. You died and rose with Jesus at the moment you confessed Him as your Lord and Savior and now you have confirmed what had happened to you through your obedience to baptism by water. Faith always obeys — congratulations! All your sins and trespasses are wiped away; they are forgiven and blotted out by the blood of Jesus forever.

The ramifications of sin are all nailed to the cross. Begin to live and enjoy your new life of victory over sin, death, disease, sickness, Satan and demons, debt, and all works of the flesh. Now you are a new man with a new boss; no more the self or Satan, but God the Holy Spirit. He will reshape your thinking to reflect your new life if allowed.

Chapter Six

THE NEW MAN

Beloved, He that is born again is a new man. "If any man be in Christ, he is a new creature: old things are passed away; behold all things are become new" (2 Corinthians 5:17). You are qualitatively new. You are holy and pure in the sight of God. Jesus has given you a new standing. Only the Holy Spirit can give birth to new life. He is the decisive factor in salvation; if you don't have the Spirit you don't belong to God. But as for you beloved, you have the Spirit:

> "Now if any man have not the Spirit of Christ, he is none of his" (Romans 8:9).

To be born again is to be born of water and of the Spirit. Born of water, you are made clean by the sprinkling of clean water and of the word of God (Ezekiel 36:25-27; John 15:3; Ephesians 5:26). Naturally born, you must be born again through the agency of the Spirit. Even though physically and externally you look the same, you are not the same on the inside; you are a brand new man. Your old body has now become the residence of the Spirit of God and the new you:

"Jesus answered, Verily, verily, I say unto thee, except a man be born of water and of the Spirit, he cannot enter into the kingdom of God" (John 3:5).

Born of the Spirit, you are born of God (John 1:3; 3:6; 1Peter 1:22-23). You are God's property, bought with the life of Jesus and sealed with His Holy Spirit. The Sprit ratifies God's ownership by sealing us with Himself. Beloved, the Spirit Himself is your seal:

"And grieve not the holy Spirit of God, whereby ye are sealed unto the day of redemption" (Ephesians 4:30; cf.1:13).

The Holy Spirit is also a pledge, the down-payment of your redemption. He is your surety or security, the guarantee that you will never be disowned or lost. God purchased you for a purpose and that purpose shall surely be fulfilled:

"Who hath also sealed us, and given the earnest of the Spirit in our hearts" (1Corinthians 1:22).

When we see Jesus face to face, it would be the happiest and glorious day for all believers including you. What has been done inside will be matched by a newly resurrected body. We will never taste death again:

"Beloved, now are we the sons of God, and it doth not yet appear what we shall be: but we know that, when he shall appear, we shall be like him; for we shall see him as he is" (1John 3:2).

At the moment, you are a new man in an old suit (old body). Old things have passed away and all things have become new. Sin is replaced with righteousness, death is replaced with life, hell is replaced with heaven, and enmity with God is replaced with love and friendship with God.

Your disposition toward God, others, and life has taken a new twist.

Beloved, you are not reformed or renovated; God has made you new through rebirth. God has declared you righteous by Christ Jesus; you don't need to worry about your past, because it has been taken care of. You are one with the Son of God, for He who sanctifies and they who are sanctified are all of one: for which cause He is not ashamed to call us brethren (Hebrews 2:11):

"For in Christ Jesus neither circumcision availeth any thing, nor uncircumcision, but a new creature" (Galatians 6:15).

"New," is what God is looking for in each of us, not reconditioned, good or better people. We must first be accepted by God if we want our services to Him and others to count for us. However, we can rejoice because we are accepted by Him. Our new man is created in righteousness and true holiness:

"Whereby are given unto us exceeding great and pre-cious promises: that by these ye might be partakers of the divine nature, having escaped the corruption that is in the world through lust" (2 Peter 1:4).

We can completely rely on God's written Word (the Bible), prayer and fellowship daily to become more and more like Christ. With a new nature we don't have to obey the old nature with its lust, and the corruption in the world. To be saved is a call to live a sanctified life and for this reason every believer is called a saint (Romans 1:6).

As a believer we have been made whole; we are cleansed from our sins by the blood of Jesus. However, the sanctifying work of the Holy Spirit will continue to the moment of our glorification. We are justified, we are been sanctified through daily renewal of the mind through the word of God by the Holy Spirit, and we shall be glorified when Jesus returns to complete the three phases of our salvation.

Through the reading and the study of His word, prayer and devotion the Spirit renews our mind until we receive the redemption of our physical bodies:

> **"and such were some of you: but ye are washed, but ye are sanctified, but ye are justified in the name of the Lord Jesus, and by the Spirit of our God" (1 Corinthians 6:11).**

Beloved, you have been separated unto God; you are set aside for God's use. As a new creature you are God's masterpiece; His trophy on display. You have been delivered from the power and influence of sin, and translated into the kingdom of God. The Kingdom (the rule of God) is within you. You are no more in darkness (ignorance and sin) but in the light (in the truth and knowledge of His Son):

> **"For we are his workmanship, created in Christ Jesus unto good works, which God hath before ordained that we should walk in them" (Ephesians 2:10).**

> **"Who hath delivered us from the power of darkness, and hath translated us into the kingdom of his dear Son" (Colossians 1:13).**

God has purged you from all sin by the blood of Jesus. You are like a lump without yeast, you are without sin, and must therefore, maintain your purity. Again, rely on the Holy Spirit for your daily victory over sin. Don't be contaminated by the fleshly lustful and sinful desires of sinners. A holy walk may require change of friends and lifestyle in general. A small leaven (sin) if not removed can contaminate the whole lump. Sin unchecked and not removed can make you think you are not born again. Your greatest enemy is sin. Sin is a reproach and a tool of the devil, watch out:

> **"Purge out therefore the old leaven, that ye may be a new lump, as ye are unleavened. For even Christ our Passover is sacrificed for us" (1Corinthians 5:7).**

Holy walk does not mean you may not sin again (that is the ideal). God has re-created you in a way that you will be able not to sin, but this will only happen if you completely surrender your will to the Holy Spirit. However, if you do sin, quickly confess and ask the Lord to wash and make you clean again:

> **"But if we walk in the light, as he is in the light, we have fellowship one with another, and the blood of Jesus Christ his Son cleanseth us from all sin.**
>
> **If we say that we have no sin, we deceive ourselves, and the truth is not in us.**
>
> **If we confess our sins, he is faithful and just to forgive us our sins, and to cleanse us from all unrighteousness" (1John 1:7-9).**

Think of the rest of your life in the space of a one day (12 hour period) one good shower is all you need, but you may have to wash your hand several times. Born again, you would not have to be reborn, however, what you may need is daily cleansing since we live in a very sinful and dirty world.

Like your natural birth, spiritual birth is once in a life time. It is not possible once born again to be unborn again. Moreover, it is impossible to re-enter your mother's womb to be reborn; so it is with spiritual birth. If it is possible, then you were not born again in the first place:

"For it is impossible for those who were once en-
lightened, and have tasted of the heavenly gift, and
were made partakers of the Holy Ghost,

And have tasted the good word of God, and the
powers of the world to come,

If they shall fall away, to renew them again unto repentance; seeing they crucify to themselves the Son
of God afresh, and put him to an open shame" (Hebrews 6:4-6).

Always remember Christ died for your sins
(1Corinthians 15:3). Don't aim at getting rich; you're
already rich, instead, aim at becoming rich in righteous
living;

"For ye know the grace of our Lord Jesus Christ,
that, though he was rich, yet for your sakes he became poor, that ye through his poverty might be
rich" (2Corinthians 8:9).

Don't serve God for what you can get out of Him; He
has already given you everything. He loaded Christ with
Himself and all that He had and gave him to you. If you
have Christ you have everything. Serve Him because you
love Him, serve Him for His grace and mercy, longsuffering
and all His daily benefits towards you, and Serve Him
because He is your Creator, Savior, and Lord:

"And ye are complete in him, which is the head of all
principality and power" (Colossians 2:10).

"In whom are hid all the treasures of wisdom and
knowledge" (Colossians 2:3).

In Christ you are full. You don't need any man to teach
you about God; God Himself lives in you by His Holy

Spirit and He shall teach you all things (1John 2:27). Every blessing God has in mind for you is in Christ, and now that Christ lives in you and you in Him you are already in the blessing. You can begin to enjoy them right now:

> "**Blessed be the God and Father of our Lord Jesus Christ, who hath blessed us with all spiritual blessings in heavenly places in Christ**" (Ephesians 1:3).

Don't waste time expecting any blessing, they are all with you, believe and walk in them. Confess how rich you are daily. Be like your Father, call forth those things that be naught as though they are (Romans 4:17). All that you and I need for this life and the life after is provided abundantly in Christ. You are in the right place at the right time. Don't put your hope in any men; don't make anyone the source of your blessings. The fullness of the Godhead bodily dwells in Christ Jesus and you are in that body:

> "**Therefore let no man glory in men. For all things are your's; Whether Paul, or Apollos, or Cephas, or the world, or life, or death, or things present, or things to come; all are your's; And ye are Christ's; and Christ is God's**" (1Corinthians 3:21-23).

Respect Pastors, your Parents, and Leaders (be that of the government or a teacher), but don't make them object of worship or hope of life (1Peter 2:17). You belong to God alone. Your Parents gave birth to you but they did not die for you; even if they could, their death could not give you all that you have in Christ. Your newness is similar to that which Adam had before the fall and that of Jesus Christ (Romans 13:14).

The new man untainted and without blemish is created after God, in Christlikeness. God sees no difference between you and Christ Jesus, His beloved Son. Begin to see and accept your newness; read what the Bible has to say about your newness and relationship with Christ. Enjoy your new you, put it on — live, talk and walk in it. You have the mind of Christ.

"And that ye put on the new man, which after God is created in righteousness and true holiness" (Ephesians 4:24).

The process of regeneration is not an act of man but of God. His work for you is complete and finished; your salvation is a done deal as far as God is concerned.

Try not to forget the words 'from' and 'into'. Remember you have been saved from something into something. You have been adorned with the beauty of Christ. You have been purified:

"Who gave himself for us, that he might redeem us from all iniquity, and purify unto himself a peculiar people, zealous of good works" (Titus 2:14).

Your old man in the regeneration was crucified with Christ, the body of sin is therefore destroyed; he is no more your boss:

"Knowing this, that our old man is crucified with him, that the body of sin might be destroyed, that henceforth we should not serve sin.

For he that is dead is freed from sin" (Romans 6:6-7).

The primary work of the Holy Spirit from now on is to transform your holy standing before God into holy living. Having sanctified you, He will continue to maintain it on a daily basis. Your life and service should reflect your holy calling and new you. God is holy; therefore, you must also be holy (1Peter 1:16). Your Heavenly Father is love, but He is also a consuming fire. Don't underestimate His hatred for sin which was vividly demonstrated in the crucifixion of His only beloved Son:

"Because it is written, be ye holy; for I am holy" (1Peter 1:16).

If Christ is in you, then you are alive forever; though your physical body may one day suffer death, the Spirit of God guarantees your resurrection from the dead. He would do the same for you as He did for Jesus (Romans 10:11):

"Ye are bought with a price; be not ye the servants of men" (1Corinthians 7:23).

Remember you are holy on account of Christ. Your faith in Him was credited or imputed to you as righteousness and that opened the way for the Holy Spirit to make you Holy; He did not just dump some holiness into you, he actually made you holy. There was a change both in standing and state. He justified and sanctified you (set aside) by grace through faith. For that reason, He now dwells in you:

"And because ye are sons, God hath sent forth the Spirit of his Son into your hearts, crying, Abba, Father.

Wherefore thou art no more a servant, but a son; and if a son, then an heir of God through Christ" (Galatians 4:6-7).

You must start working out your own Salvation so that you can win for yourself some medals on that day. The faith and obedience of Christ won for you access to the Father and entrance into heaven. Now, you must put your faith to work by exercising obedience and holy living, and through that, win for yourself the incorruptible crown before the Lord, and the Holy angels on that day (1Corinthians 9:24-

27). You must press toward the mark for the prize of the high calling of God in Christ (Philippians 3:14). People must praise God because of the purity of life and your love for others:

> **"Wherefore, my beloved, as ye have always obeyed, not as in my presence only, but now much more in my absence, work out your own salvation with fear and trembling" (Philippians 2:12).**

You are now a member of God's household and a joint heir with Christ. The Holy Spirit has baptized you into the body of Christ. You are connected by the Spirit to millions of believers worldwide (1Corinthians 12:13). You have joined the millions who serve God out of a pure heart. True believers everywhere are your brothers and sisters. You are a member of the church of God; I don't mean the denominational church of God, but rather the Church universal (Acts 20:18):

> **"But ye are a chosen generation, a royal priesthood, an holy nation, a peculiar people; that ye should shew forth the praises of him who hath called you out of darkness into his marvelous light" (1 Peter 2:9).**

> **"For ye are all children of God by faith in Christ Jesus.**
>
> **For as many of you as have been baptized into Christ have put on Christ.**
>
> **There is neither Jew nor Greek, there is neither bond nor free, there is neither male nor female: for ye are all one in Christ Jesus.**

And if ye be Christ's, then are ye Abraham's seed, and heirs according to the promise" (Galatians 3:26-29).

Together with the rest of the people of God, the Holy Spirit is building a house for the habitation of God:

"Ye also, as lively stones, are built up a spiritual house, an holy priesthood, to offer up spiritual sacrifices, acceptable to God by Jesus Christ" (2Peter 2:5).

In conclusion, what has happened to you is more than just cultivating good habits or being religious. It is a miracle, a supernatural work of God covering spirit, soul, and body; it is beyond the reach and capability of man. You must renew your mind daily on all that you have learned about your new nature; they will surely keep you from sin. Sanctification is the renewal of the mind by the Holy Spirit through the word of God. Daily feeding on the spiritual food of God's word is a must as a newly born baby in Christ. Your spiritual growth depends on your willingness and submissiveness to the Holy Spirit.

Chapter Seven

THE NEW BOSS

You are under a new management; seated upon the throne of your new heart and spirit is your new boss, the Spirit of Jesus Christ. Jesus purposely sent Him to be in His beloved children; to work in and through them. He is, therefore, in you to renew your mind, and also work through you as a witness to the world by your life and service.

While on earth, Jesus could not be in all places at the same time; He was very limited. But now that He is on the throne in heaven, exalted, and having received and sent forth His Holy Spirit, He can be everywhere at the same time (Acts 2:33).

"Even the Spirit of truth; whom the world cannot receive, because it seeth him not, neither knoweth him: but ye know him; for he dwelleth with you, and shall be in you" (John 14:17).

Christians carry Jesus with them wherever they go, and wherever a Christian is, there He is as well. All those who are in Christ are also in the Spirit and vice versa:

"But when the Comforter is come, whom I will send unto you from the Father, even the Spirit of truth, which proceedeth from the Father, he shall testify of me:

And ye also shall bear witness, because ye have been with me from the beginning" (John 15:26-27).

————————————

"But ye shall receive power, after that the Holy Ghost is come upon you: and ye shall be witnesses unto me both in Jerusalem, and in all Judaea, and in Samaria, and unto the uttermost part of the earth" (Acts 1:8).

You must be cognizant of His presence, having been born of Him, He resides to complete what He has started, and that is to present you holy, unblameable, and unreproveable in the sight of God. His character is His name, Holy; for this reason, He is called the Spirit of holiness. He is the one who sanctifies us through the Son (Romans 15:16). He lives in all believers and all believers live in Him. He came in the moment you accepted Jesus Christ as Lord and Savior and He will dwell with you forever. He is the gift from Jesus to all those who are born again:

"What? know ye not that your body is the temple of the Holy Ghost which is in you, which ye have of God, and ye are not your own?" (1 Corinthians 6:19).

The Holy Spirit has a job to do in all of us; there is a world to be changed and a people to be saved. It is, therefore, extremely important as a Christian, to yield your will to Him, and to cooperate fully with Him. This enables Him to accomplish the purpose for which He has been sent. All His vast resources are available to you if only you let Him. He is your source of power for a life of service to God and fellow man:

> "And he that keepeth his commandments dwelleth in him, and he in him. And hereby we know that he abideth in us, by the Spirit which he hath given us" (1John 3:24).

To be born again, means, new man with a new boss; the Holy Spirit is your new boss forever. Before, you did that which was pleasing to you; that lifestyle is over. You must now live your life before God by walking in the Spirit. You are required to obey and do all that He may require of you. He is in you, and in the world to glorify Jesus, so permit Him to do so:

> "For as many as are led by the Spirit of God, they are the sons of God" (Romans 8:14).

Your primary responsibility is to train your ears to listen and to do those things which are pleasing to Him. He has a mind, heart, and will of His own. Probably, what you should do foremost is to ask Him to empty you and fill you with Himself. Ask Him repeatedly to take full possession of you (Acts 6-7). Beware of grieving Him and do not quench Him (Ephesians 4:30).

Nothing you do will please God unless it is done on the impulse of His Spirit. Don't waist time and money doing anything for God, unless He instructs you to do so. Remember, God is the possessor of heaven and earth, by Himself He has no need, so be very careful in your relationship with Him. Don't work to impress Him, just be the obedient child:

> "For he that soweth to his flesh shall of the flesh reap corruption; but he that soweth to the Spirit shall of the Spirit reap life everlasting" (Galatians 6:8).

Being in Christ, the flesh is crucified together with the affections and lusts. You should no longer bear the fruits of the sinful old self, but the new:

> **"But the fruit of the Spirit is love, joy, peace, long-suffering, gentleness, goodness, faith, Meekness, temperance: against such there is no law"** (Galatians 5:22-23).

The Holy Spirit is now your true friend forever. He is absolutely dependable and trustworthy. You can leave all decision makings to Him and you will never go wrong. He is the Spirit that came from Jesus who is the Truth. He is the one who continually assures the believer of his position as a child of God. Inside you, He is closer to you than anybody and readily available. He is never too busy, asleep, or away on a journey.

You are no longer in the flesh, but in the Spirit. Never say I am just a human being, because you are not. You are a spirit being. For the Spirit of God lives in you, and if the Spirit lives in you, then you are one with the Spirit. It is no longer you that liveth, but Christ who lives in you by His Spirit.

In the regeneration, the Spirit added to your human nature a divine nature in the same way He added to Jesus' divine nature a human nature at His incarnation. You are therefore a peculiar person. Born of God, you are a citizen of heaven. You possess dual citizenship, which is that of heaven and of the earth. Remember, you also have two birth certificates; your birthright is now natural and spiritual birth. You are very special to God, and must see yourself so. The Spirit in you is the proof of your sonship. Because you are child, you must expect discipline when you do wrong:

> **"For whom the Lord loveth he chasteneth, and scourgeth every son whom he receiveth.**

If ye endure chastening, God dealeth with you as with sons; for what son is he whom the father chasteneth not?

But if ye be without chastisement, whereof all are partakers, then are ye bastards, and not sons" (Hebrews 12:6-8).

It is a great honor that God has wrought in and upon all believers by allowing His Holy Spirit to live in the vessels of clay. The glory and power of the highest residing in human beings is love at its highest. What a privilege and honor to fallen man! Adam lost the glory; Jesus found it and brought it back to us, Amen. Christ in us is the hope of glory. Because we have the Holy Spirit in us, we have the mind of Christ and that of God. As our teacher, He teaches us all we need to know about Jesus and God the Father:

"But the anointing which ye have received of him abideth in you, and ye need not that any man teach you: but as the same anointing teacheth you of all things, and is truth, and is no lie, and even as it hath taught you, ye shall abide in him" (1John 2:27).

The Holy Spirit is the anointing of God in and upon your life, so that you can walk as He walked and talk as He talked. You know and possess all things because of Him (1John 2:20). You are set for a fruitful Christian life; if you rely on Him, your daily life will be full of miracles.

God is the source of our redemption, Jesus is the means of our redemption, and the Holy Spirit is the dispenser of our redemption. Redemption was given by the Father, but there was no way it could get to us because of the sin problem, but Jesus bought it for us and the Holy Spirit brought it down to you.

As far as God's dealing with man is concerned, the order of divine performance has always been: all things come from the Father, through the Son, and by the Holy Spirit. It is the same for all that goes to the Father from us; for example, our prayers and services must be from the Spirit, through Jesus, and to the Father.

Chapter Eight

INNER CONFLICT

Sadly, in the regeneration, the old man was not eradicated or renewed. Sin, though powerless, therefore remains in the flesh. This means, every Christian has two natures: the old sinful nature (the old man or self) and the new nature (new man or self) received at rebirth. Whatever God does is good and is full of meaning and purpose; we need not question His integrity. Faith always obeys even if it transcends the natural mind. Love believes all things and is demonstrated in obedience. "If you love me, keep my commandments," Jesus said (John 14:15). The grace of God is sufficient under any trial; His strength is made perfect in weakness (2Corinthians 12:9):

"But we have this treasure in earthen vessels, that the excellency of the power may be of God, and not of us" (2Corinthians 4:7).

As a result of the two natures living in the same house, there is constant struggle between the Spirit and the flesh. The new man mirrors Christlikeness and imitates God. The old man or flesh is a slave to sin and imitates the devil. The two are antagonistic to each other:

"Now the works of the flesh are manifest, which are these; Adultery, fornication, uncleanness, lasciviousness,

Idolatry, witchcraft, hatred, variance, emulations, wrath, strife, seditions, heresies,

Envying, murders, drunkenness, revellings, and such like: of the which I tell you before, as I have also told you in time past, that they which do such things shall not inherit the kingdom of God.

But the fruit of the Spirit is love, joy, peace, longsuffering, gentleness, goodness, faith, meekness, temperance: against such there is no law

And they that are Christ's have crucified the flesh with the affection and lust" (Galatians 5:19-24).

They that are Christ's have crucified the flesh (old man); they must consider themselves dead to the world with its lust and alive unto God. "If we live in the Spirit, let us also walk in the Spirit" (Galatians 5:25). As a Christian you must reckon yourself dead unto sin, but alive unto God through the Lord Jesus Christ. He that is dead with Christ is freed from sin; sin has no dominion over him. Jesus died in our place to put away sin; we, too, must consider ourselves dead to sin and alive to righteousness.

Just like the Apostle Paul we should be able to say, "I live by the faith of Jesus Christ." We must not allow the decaying body with its dethroned occupant to actively interfere with our new life in Christ:

"I am crucified with Christ: nevertheless I live; yet not I, but Christ liveth in me: and the life which I now live in the flesh I live by the faith of the Son of

God, who loved me, and gave himself for me" (Galatians 2:20).

The arrival of the new man means the old man is no longer needed. The new man replaces the old man in the same way the last Adam (Jesus) replaces the first Adam (1 Corinthian 15:45). The old sinful nature is no longer in control. The new has arrived; the old self must be put away for good. If you want to live a consistent holy life then you must be whole heartedly and completely yielded to the Holy Spirit. Your will, heart, and mind must be made subject to the Spirit at all times:

"That ye put off concerning the former conversation the old man, which is corrupt according to the deceitful lusts;

And be renewed in the spirit of your mind" (Ephesians 4:22-23).

The mind is the battle ground in every believer. The mind is to the soul just as the heart is to the spirit. Heart and mind must be full of faith, leaving no space for the devil. The will must be made subject to the Holy Spirit who reigns over your spirit. As awareness of the new standing and state in Christ grows, the old man with his evil desires fades out until we become like Christ in character and service. Fact translates into power as we increase in understanding and in the knowledge of Jesus and what He has accomplished for us.

Honestly, there is not enough room for both the new and old self in the life of the born again. To put it bluntly, the old man is dead as far as control and influence are concerned; he was crucified with Christ at rebirth. The new man should be growing stronger and stronger by each passing day. These are facts not hypothesis; we must renew our mind daily by feeding on the word of God and trusting the Spirit of God to grant victory day by day.

Every Christian, till we leave this earth, is expected to read daily, understand and grow in knowledge of our Lord Jesus Christ and all that the Bible has to say. You must not pay any attention to the old man no matter what:

> **"And that ye put on the new man, which after God is created in righteousness and true holiness" (Ephesians 4:24).**

Remember, Baptism is symbolic of death and resurrection; the old life was buried, and we resurrected to a whole newness of life. Believers are dead to sin:

> **"Knowing this, that our old man is crucified with him, that the body of sin might be destroyed, that henceforth we should not serve sin.**
>
> **For he that is dead is freed from sin.**
>
> **Now if we be dead with Christ, we believe that we shall also live with him:**
>
> **Knowing that Christ being raised from the dead dieth no more; death hath no more dominion over him. For in that he died, he died unto sin once: but in that he liveth, he liveth unto God.**
>
> **Likewise reckon ye also yourselves to be dead indeed unto sin, but alive unto God through Jesus Christ our Lord.**
>
> **Let not sin therefore reign in your mortal body, that ye should obey it in the lusts thereof.**
>
> **Neither yield ye your members as instruments of unrighteousness unto sin: but yield yourselves unto**

God, as those that are alive from the dead, and your members as instruments of righteousness unto God" (Romans 6:6-13).

Led by the Holy Spirit is the guarantee for victory over the flesh. If you put the old man in check; Satan can't entice you into sin. You don't need any law if you abide under the command of the Spirit; the Spirit is the Law. The law of God was not made for the righteous, but for sinners. If we walk by the Spirit there is no condemnation whatsoever:

"Knowing this, that the law is not made for a righteous man, but for the lawless and disobedient, for the ungodly and for sinners, for unholy and profane, for murderers of fathers and murderers of mothers, for manslayers" (1 Timothy 1:9).

As a warning, never underestimate the old man; no believer by himself can win any battle with the old man unless by the Spirit: "Trust and obey for there is no other way" as a hymnist, once wrote, is true for every believer. You have God the Father, God the Son and God the Holy Spirit on your side; there is no way you can be a loser if you trust and obey:

"But if ye be led of the Spirit, ye are not under the law" (Galatians 5:18).

The flesh draws it strength from a world that is estranged from God and therefore earthly minded. The new man is from heaven and draws his strength from God and is heaven minded. The battle between the two will only cease after death (physical).

As a new born baby, "you must desire the sincere milk of the word of God that you may grow thereby" (1Peter 2:2). You must grow in your understanding of what the will of God is in every given situation (2 Peter 3:18). While you are in the grace, grow in the knowledge of your savior and Lord Jesus Christ. Walk in newness of life (Romans 6:4).

Exercise to know Him more and more. Seize the love of God and desire to be like Him. Again, read your Bible and pray daily. Ask Jesus to strengthen you by His Spirit and to keep you from temptation. Take the pain to grow your faith. Make conscious effort to know God intimately and personally. Ask the Holy Spirit to lead you to a Bible believing teaching fellowship or Church if you don't have one already. Don't be concerned about the size of the group and the place of meeting whether it is state of art or shack.

Remember, anytime you try to do well, the evil one through the flesh will try to tempt you to do the opposite. Be therefore vigilant and alert. Don't neglect fellowship with other believers. Iron sharpens iron; there is mutual benefit when believers fellowship one with another: "For where two or three are gathered together in my name, there am I in the midst of them" (Matthew 18:20).

Chapter Nine

More Than Conquerors

You must not be afraid of losing your salvation. It is secured in Christ and in God. No one can pluck you out of the hand of God, not even yourself. No man can separate you from the love of God. We (Christians) are blessed, and there is nothing anybody can do about it, not even ourselves:

> "Nay, in all these things we are more than conquerors through him that loved us.
>
> For I am persuaded, that neither death, nor life, nor angels, nor principalities, nor powers, nor things present, nor things to come,
>
> nor height, nor depth, nor any other creature, shall be able to separate us from the love of God, which is in Christ Jesus our Lord" (Romans 8:37-39).

In all things, be it job loss, lost relationship, sickness or suffering, God promises to be with us and never to leave or forsake us. He promises to deliver us from them all. "Even though we walk through the shadow of death we shall fear no evil" (Psalm 23). We can say with Brother Job, "I know that my redeemer liveth" (Job 19:25). Jesus, our great high Priest in heaven, is praying and interceding for us. The Holy Spirit in us is standing in for Him on earth till He comes He comes to take His own. Living inside each of us, He guarantees our victory no matter what.

God the Father is all out for you. He can't wait to see us when our race in this life is over. Again, with us is an invincible force. No demon on earth or in hell can play games with you. Jesus is the head and we are His body. God our Father has put all things under the feet of Jesus and under our feet since we are His body (Ephesians 2:20-23). His name is your authority and power; at the name of Jesus every knee shall bow of things in heaven, in earth, and under the earth (Philippians 2:9-11). No weapon that is formed against you shall prosper. God is on your side and if God be for you, who can be against you? You must not be afraid of what man can do to you because of Him; after all, man can only kill your body, but can't go beyond that (Matthew 10:28).

Death has no power over you; to you, physical death means to be reclothed with your resurrected body; it means to have a body like that of Jesus after His resurrection:

"Now this I say, brethren, that flesh and blood cannot inherit the kingdom of God; neither doth corruption inherit incorruption.

Behold, I shew you a mystery; We shall not all sleep, but we shall all be changed,

In a moment, in the twinkling of an eye, at the last trump: for the trumpet shall sound, and the dead shall be raised incorruptible, and we shall be changed.

For this corruptible must put on incorruption, and this mortal must put on immortality.

So when this corruptible shall have put on incorruption, and this mortal shall have put on immortality, then shall be brought to pass the saying that is written, Death is swallowed up in victory.

O death, where is thy sting? O grave, where is thy victory? The sting of death is sin; and the strength of sin is the law.

But thanks be to God, which giveth us the victory through our Lord Jesus Christ.

Therefore, my beloved brethren, be ye stedfast, unmoveable, always abounding in the work of the Lord, forasmuch as ye know that your labor is not in vain in the Lord" (1 Corinthians 15:50-58).

You are secured in Jesus as Jesus is secured in God. Whether your salvation probably just took place or years ago, your heavenly Father knew well ahead of time and predestined you to glorification through the process of justification, and sanctification by His Spirit:

"For whom he did foreknow, he also did predestinate to be conformed to the image of his Son, that he might be the firstborn among many brethren.

Moreover whom he did predestinate, them he also called: and whom he called, them he also justified: and whom he justified, them he also glorified" (Romans 8:29-30).

You were chosen in Christ to be made like Christ before the world was made (2 Timothy 1:9). "Foreknow' means

"before," or whom God knew before He predetermined
their end. In that dateless past when God chose Christ for
us, He also chose all those who are to be saved in Him.
Again, the purpose of our calling is to be a holy nation, the
holy people of God (Ephesians 1:4-5).

God chose you, you did not choose Him. He saved
you; you did not save yourself. It was not by your own
works or effort that gave you new birth; God did so by His
own sovereign grace through the faith of Jesus Christ by
His Spirit:

> "Ye have not chosen me, but I have chosen you, and
> ordained you, that ye should go and bring forth fruit,
> and that your fruit should remain: that whatsoever
> ye shall ask of the Father in my name, he may give it
> you" (John 15:16).

> "Who hath saved us, and called us with an holy call-
> ing, not according to our works, but according to his
> own purpose and grace, which was given us in Christ
> Jesus before the world began" (2 Timothy 1:9).

In the same way, you are not kept saved and safe by
your own effort, but that of Christ and His Spirit; you
are being kept daily by the power of His word and the
indwelling Spirit:

> "Not by works of righteousness which we have
> done, but according to his mercy he saved us, by the
> washing of regeneration, and renewing of the Holy
> Ghost" (Titus 3:5).

> "In hope of eternal life, which God, that cannot lie,
> promised before the world began" (Titus 1:2).

Put on therefore the whole armor of God like a soldier ready for battle. Satan, who controls the mind and hearts of unbelievers, will exercise all that is within his power to entice you through the deceitfulness of riches to sin or get you dissuaded from your holy calling. Stand strong and resist him with the power and might of the Holy Spirit. Do all you can to speak the truth at all times; be grounded in the word of God, be desirous to live holy before God and man.

Witness; tell others about your faith. The sooner you let friends and family know about your being a Christian, the better for you. They may unknowingly help you to maintain a consistent Christian lifestyle. Their criticism and rebuke will serve as a protective shield against the devil by helping you stay in line.

I pray that "the very God of peace will sanctify you wholly; and that your whole spirit, soul and body be preserved blameless unto the coming of our Lord Jesus Christ" (1 Thessalonians 5:23). Hope to see you in heaven some day. Share this book with all your loved ones who are not saved. This book is written for them too. The peace of God be with your spirit Amen.

Chapter Ten

YOU SHALL BE GLORIFIED

It is important that all prophesies be fulfilled. Christ will definitely return to earth to be glorified in those who believed in him and them to be glorified by Him. It will be the great union of the groom with his bride. That day is coming, it won't be long:

"When he shall come to be glorified in his saints, and to be admired in all them that believe (because our testimony among you was believed) in that day" (2 Thessalonians 1:10).

On that day we shall be clothed with a new body just like His; we shall be like Him. Our salvation which begun with the creation of the new man will be completed. Justification and sanctification will be dressed in glorification. The new man will receive a new suit. This instantaneous work of our redemption by the Holy Spirit is what we call glorification:

"Beloved, now are we the sons of God, and it doth not yet appear what we shall be: but we know that, when he shall appear, we shall be like him; for we shall see him as he is" (1 John 3:2).

God, who cannot lie, would definitely bring what He had begun in justification and in sanctification to glorification. Glorification is the very determinate end for all those who are elected of God:

"Being confident of this very thing, that he which hath begun a good work in you will perform it until the day of Jesus Christ" (Philippians 1:5).

The purpose of our being chosen in Christ is to be glorified. Glorification completes our transformation into the image and likeness of the Son of God. We shall be exactly like Him. We shall be saved from the presence and power of sin to sin no more. We shall not be able to sin:

"For whom he did foreknow, he also did predestinate to be conformed to the image of his Son that he might be the firstborn among many brethren.

Moreover whom he did predestinate, them he also called: and whom he called, them he also justified: and whom he justified, them he also glorified" (Romans 8:29-30; cf. 1Peter 5:10).

At the moment, what the Holy Spirit is doing in all of us is changing us day by day into the very character of Jesus, but on that day, the renewing of the mind and likeness in thought, word and deed would be completed. Let us, therefore, continue to work out our own salvation; meaning, stay connected to the faith of Jesus Christ with great reverence. Show proof of your salvation in good works. Be zealous for good work, which was our original vocation before the fall:

"But we all, with open face beholding as in a glass the glory of the Lord, are changed into the same image from glory to glory, even as by the Spirit of the Lord" (2Corinthians 3:18).

Good works for a Christian only counts before God after Salvation. We can't work up to salvation, but can work from salvation. To "work out," does not mean, "do it yourself." It means, depend on God the Holy Spirit to do the work of God through you:

"Wherefore, my beloved, as ye have always obeyed, not as in my presence only, but now much more in my absence, work out your own salvation with fear and trembling.

For it is God which worketh in you both to will and to do of his good pleasure" (Philippians 2:12-13).

Salvation from start to finish is all the work of God (even though it is true that you played a part). For example, you repented, and you opened your mouth to accept Jesus as Lord; however, they were all works of grace. You were enabled as undeserving servants to do them. We must have the mind of John the Baptist in everything we do in the name of God by repeating after him, "we are not worthy" (John 1:17). Salvation, beginning to finish is all the work of God. Whatever service we do for God or on His behalf should be a reciprocal of His love for us.

No amount of sufferings endured can be compared with the glory yet to be revealed in and on us. Therefore, endure hardship as a good soldier of the Lord, knowing that your hard work would not be in vain:

"For I reckon that the sufferings of this present time are not worthy to be compared with the glory which shall be revealed in us" (Romans 8:18).

Can you imagine life without Christ and the hope of salvation; it would be life without meaning and catastrophic. But thanks to God, there is meaning to life and a purpose to life. Soon the sons of God would be glorified and creation also would be free:

"For the earnest expectation of the creature waiteth for the manifestation of the sons of God.

For the creature was made subject to vanity, not willingly, but by reason of him who hath subjected the same in hope,

Because the creature itself also shall be delivered from the bondage of corruption into the glorious liberty of the children of God.

For we know that the whole creation groaneth and travaileth in pain together until now" (Romans 8:19-22).

At the moment, creation is in pain waiting to be freed; believers, including ourselves, are also anxiously waiting for that day. Had it not been for the many that are yet to be saved, (which necessitate that we preach the Gospel to them also), I can boldly say, I am ready to depart to my Lord. Beloved, there is hope – much hope for everyone in this world:

"And not only they, but ourselves also, which have the firstfruits of the Spirit, even we ourselves groan within ourselves, waiting for the adoption, to wit, the redemption of our body" (Romans 8:23).

I believe at this stage you are well equipped for the rest of your Christian life. There is no more doubt about your salvation, look to the brighter days ahead. You also know the Holy Spirit dwells in you and goes everywhere with you. He is your closest neighbor, closer than your very skin. Together you are an invincible force.

Finally, Beloved, tell your story; you have the opportunity now to personalize this book. I believe the crown of this book is your story. Your children, grandchildren, and great grandchildren may want to know how you became a Christian. Maybe it was a miracle in itself how this book got into your hands, no one will know unless you tell it.

May the grace of our Lord Jesus Christ, the love of God and fellowship of the Holy Spirit be with you now and forevermore.

Chapter Eleven

My Testimony of How
I Became Saved

_____

_____

_____

_____

_____

_____

_____

_____

_____

_____

_____

_____

_____

_____

_____

_____

_____

_____

_____

_____

Printed in the United States
204696BV00004B/1-180/P